It was hard to call them friends.

Business associates would have been a mischaracterization. "Acquaintances?" Rose offered, closing her eyes for a moment against the tingle his touch sent through her.

There was a smile in his voice. "That's a start."

Warren didn't move his hand from her face. And she didn't want him to.

She realized she'd been holding her breath. "A start?"

"Well," said Warren, "technically you could say we already had a start, a few weeks ago."

She swallowed. "You could also say that was an aberration. A moment of weakness."

Warren laughed and reached out, putting his hands on her shoulders. "Or maybe just basic attraction," he said, looking into her eyes before he drew her into a kiss...

Dear Reader,

No month better suits Silhouette Romance than February. For it celebrates that breathless feeling of first love, the priceless experiences and memories that come with a longtime love and the many hopes and dreams that give a couple's life together so much meaning. At Silhouette Romance, our writers try to capture all these feelings in their timeless tales…and this month's lineup is no exception.

Our PERPETUALLY YOURS promotion continues this month with a charming tale from Sandra Paul. In *Domesticating Luc* (#1802) a dog trainer gets more than she bargained for when she takes on an unruly puppy and his very obstinate and irresistible owner. Beloved author Judy Christenberry returns to the lineup with *Honeymoon Hunt* (#1803)—a madcap adventure in which two opposites pair up to find their parents who have eloped, but instead wind up on a tight race to the finish line, er, altar! In *A Dash of Romance* (#1804) Elizabeth Harbison creates the perfect recipe for love when she pairs a self-made billionaire with a spirited waitress. Cathie Linz rounds out the offerings with *Lone Star Marine* (#1805). Part of her MEN OF HONOR series, this poignant romance features a wounded soldier who craves only the solitude to heal, and finds that his lively and beautiful neighbor just might be the key to the future he hadn't dreamed possible.

As always, be sure to return next month when Alice Sharpe concludes our PERPETUALLY YOURS promotion.

Happy reading.

Ann Leslie Tuttle
Associate Senior Editor

Please address questions and book requests to:
Silhouette Reader Service
U.S.: 3010 Walden Ave., P.O. Box 1325, Buffalo, NY 14269
Canadian: P.O. Box 609, Fort Erie, Ont. L2A 5X3

Elizabeth Harbison

A Dash of Romance

SILHOUETTE *Romance*®

Published by Silhouette Books

America's Publisher of Contemporary Romance

To Paige and Jack with love from Mommy

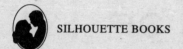

SILHOUETTE BOOKS

ISBN 0-373-19804-3

A DASH OF ROMANCE

Copyright © 2006 by Elizabeth Harbison

This edition published by arrangement with Harlequin Books S.A.

® and TM are trademarks of Harlequin Books S.A., used under license.
Trademarks indicated with ® are registered in the United States Patent
and Trademark Office, the Canadian Trade Marks Office and in other
countries.

Visit Silhouette Books at www.eHarlequin.com

Printed in U.S.A.

Books by Elizabeth Harbison

Silhouette Romance

A Groom for Maggie #1239
Wife without a Past #1258
Two Brothers and a Bride #1286
True Love Ranch #1323
*Emma and the Earl #1410
*Plain Jane Marries the Boss #1416
*Annie and the Prince #1423
*His Secret Heir #1528
A Pregnant Proposal #1553
Princess Takes a Holiday #1643
The Secret Princess #1713
Taming of the Two #1790
A Dash of Romance #1804

*Cinderella Brides

Silhouette Special Edition

Drive Me Wild #1476
Midnight Cravings #1539
How To Get Your Man #1685
Diary of a Domestic Goddess
  #1727

Silhouette Books

Lone Star Country Club
Mission Creek Mother-To-Be

ELIZABETH HARBISON

has always been an avid reader. After devouring the Nancy Drew and Trixie Belden series in grade school, she moved on to the suspense of Mary Stewart, Dorothy Eden and Daphne du Maurier, just to name a few. From there it was a natural progression to writing, although early efforts have been securely hidden away in the back of a closet.

After authoring three cookbooks, Elizabeth turned her hand to writing romances and hasn't looked back. Her second book for Silhouette Romance, *Wife without a Past*, was a 1998 finalist for the Romance Writers of America's prestigious RITA® Award in the Best Traditional Romance category.

Elizabeth lives in Maryland with her husband, John, daughter Mary Paige and son Jack, as well as two dogs, Bailey and Zuzu. She loves to hear from readers and you can write to her at c/o Box 1636, Germantown, MD 20875.

ARTICHOKE SALAD WITH CARAMELIZED SHALLOT AND CHAMPAGNE TRUFFLE VINAIGRETTE

Serves 4

3 tbsp of extra virgin olive oil
3 shallots, sliced and tossed with a little brown sugar
1 large garlic clove, minced fine
1 tbsp lemon juice
1 tbsp brut champagne or sherry
2 tbsp champagne vinegar
3 tbsp white truffle oil
Pinch of salt
Freshly ground black pepper
2 cups artichoke hearts, marinated in oil and drained
1 cup baby arugula, washed and drained

Heat olive oil in a large heavy-bottomed pan over medium-high heat. Add the sliced shallots and sauté slowly until they start to caramelize. Once the shallots start to achieve a deep amber color, toss in the garlic and sauté for one minute.

Remove pan from heat.

Whisk together lemon juice, champagne or sherry and champagne vinegar. While whisking briskly, slowly drizzle in the white truffle oil. Add salt and a grind or two of black pepper.

Put the artichokes into the pan with the shallots and garlic and heat very gently over low heat, tossing the artichokes to fully integrate the flavor of the shallots and garlic.

Remove artichokes, shallots and garlic, placing them in a decorative bowl. Pour the champagne and truffle oil mixture over them. Toss again.

Add arugula. Toss again.

Serve warm or chilled.

Prologue

Twenty-Five Years Ago

"What a shame," said Virginia Porter, director of the Barrie Home for Children, looking at the little girls who had lost their parents in a car crash just one week ago. The little angels were sleeping now, but they had spent more restless hours awake and crying than Virginia could count. She'd walked the floors with them every night. If any of her hair had remained brunette at the beginning of the week, it was all gray now. "So young to be all alone in the world. It's a terrible, terrible shame."

The air conditioner kicked on, sending, as if on cue, a cold breeze into the room.

"Do you think we'll be able to keep them together?" Sister Gladys asked, kneading her hands in front of her. "I can't bear the idea of separating them."

Virginia sighed. "Of course we'll continue to try and find some next of kin, but it's not looking hopeful at this point. We'll have to start thinking about placement." She frowned, already worried about how little control she might have over the matter. Like Sister Gladys, Virginia wanted to keep the girls together, but it would be hard to refuse a good home to one if the parents wanted just one child. At least the girls were young enough, at thirteen or fourteen months, that they probably wouldn't remember any of this later. "We'll do the very best that we can."

"They'll need each other, Miss Porter," Sister Gladys insisted. If possible, she was even more tender-hearted than Virginia. "They've lost their parents so horribly, so suddenly. Surely we can make sure they keep each other. Please."

The little redheaded girl, Rose, stirred in her sleep and Virginia bent down and stroked her hair to soothe her back to sleep. If she woke up, she'd cry… They could already tell that Rose was the most sensitive one of the three.

"We'll try." Virginia said softly, smoothing the child's copper curls as she spoke. "I promise you, we'll try."

Chapter One

"Warren Harker, age, forty-one, height six feet two, hair, black, eyes, blue, educated at Stanford, but got his master's from Harvard Business School."

Rose Tilden listened incredulously as her boss, Marta Serragno, of Serragno Catering, listed the attributes of the man who had hired them to cater his party tonight.

"Has worked in real estate development and construction since 1988, established Harker Companies in 1992. Likes his meat rare, his business cold and his women hot. Bank portfolio, four hundred and twenty-seven million, give or take a million." Marta licked her lips. "And soon he's going to be mine." She turned her dark eyes on Rose. "You can count on it."

"You sound pretty sure of yourself," Rose commented.

"Do you doubt me?"

Frequently, Rose thought. But there was no point in arguing with Marta. It wouldn't end until she felt she'd won. Might as well give in to her early on. "Never."

"Wise girl." Marta tapped her index finger against her temple. "That's the right answer."

"Although, if you ask me…" Rose went on. Sometimes she was unable to stop herself from giving her opinion. Her sister, Lily, said it was her red hair that made her fiery that way. "We could do with a little less real estate development and a little more fixing up of what already exists."

Marta gave her a chilly look. "I do hope you don't plan on saying that to Harker."

"Not unless he asks." She'd never been shy about giving her opinion. Lily also kept telling her she needed to learn to *zip it,* because that red headed fire was going to get her into trouble, but every time she tried, she failed.

This was particularly bad in her line of work, since she was supposed to be nice and accommodating with the client and their guests, even in the face of sexual advances (which happened a lot) or complaints that were clearly concocted with the aim of getting free service (which happened even more frequently). Rose was amazed how often the richer clients tried to get something for free. Three years into the business, Rose had learned several strange truths, and one was that the wealthier the clients, the cheaper they tended to be.

And the cheaper they were, the meaner they tended to be.

Rose had trouble with that, but Marta was just fine with it. The richer the better, she didn't care.

"Frankly, my dear," she said to Rose, "you're not going to have any sort of conversation with our client, so the idea of him asking your opinion on inner city refurbishment is out of the question."

Rose gave a short nod. Marta was really such a jerk. If she weren't so ridiculous, Rose might occasionally feel offended by her slings and arrows.

"Now," Marta went on. "Did you make that artichoke salad everyone likes so much?"

"Eight pounds of it." Rose pointed to the large bowl she'd been working on for the past hour. She knew why Marta wanted the lemon artichoke salad. It was one of Rose's specialties. As a matter of fact, it was one of the dishes that tended to…well, people *thought* it had some sort of aphrodisiacal properties.

Clearly, Marta was looking for magic.

"You did it…" Marta gave a small, tight smile. "The usual way, right?"

Rose held a smile back. Marta was so transparent. "I *always* do it the same way," she assured her.

"Excellent." Marta turned her attention back to the

gorgeous man in the parlor of the large hotel suite. "I'll definitely be having a bowl of that tonight. Even though I hate artichokes."

Rose stopped working and looked at her boss. "Marta, if you hate artichokes, don't eat it."

"If anything they say about that dish is true, I'm going to eat it."

"Not everything *they* say is true."

"Honey, if I eat it, the stories had *better* be true," Marta said, in a voice that could have been jesting or bitterly serious.

Rose shrugged. "You haven't even met Warren Harker yet. What if he's a dud?"

Marta fixed a cold dark eye on her. "Number one: I have met him, although briefly. And number two: if he is a dud, he's a dud worth four hundred and twenty-seven million." She pressed her thin red lips together. "For that, I might have to learn to love artichokes. Wait a minute." She touched her finger to her chin. "Maybe all that matters is if *he* likes artichokes."

Rose shook her head and wordlessly went to assemble the silver chargers of cheese by region. Marta didn't like cheese. She didn't like fish. She didn't like any vegetables. She didn't like sweets. In fact, Rose had rarely seen her put anything in her mouth at all. Why she was still in the catering business was a mystery.

After all, she'd only inherited the business. Her

second husband—or was it her third?—had left it to her when he'd died several years back. In that time, to her credit, Marta had kept the business going and had even upped its profile. But she'd never once shown any interest in food. She was just ruthlessly ambitious, and willing to succeed in any area that would allow her to prosper, both financially and socially.

So she'd succeeded in the catering business by hiring the best people and running the operation with an iron fist. So what if she couldn't cook? In true Henry Ford fashion, she'd simply hired someone who could.

Rose.

Rose, along with her sister, Lily, had grown up in the Barrie Children's Home in Brooklyn. The two had spent some of their time in foster care, all fairly good experiences, but as they'd grown older they'd spent more and more time at the orphanage. People didn't want to foster older children as much as younger ones.

When they were sixteen, though, they learned that their first foster mother had died, leaving her meager estate to the girls so that they could go to vocational school and learn a trade.

Rose had gone to culinary school, while her sister had studied hotel management. Now, while Rose worked as an assistant caterer for Marta, one of the most prominent caterers in New York, Lily was a concierge in one of New York's most exclusive boutique hotels, the Montclaire.

"How's it going in here?" a small, twitchy man with a dark comb-over and black-rimmed glasses asked. "Is everything on schedule?"

"It certainly is, Mr. Potts," Marta cooed. "You go tell your boss everything is just fine. In fact, maybe he'd like to come in here and—" she gave a coy smile "—sample my wares."

Mr. Potts raised his eyebrows so high his glasses slid down his nose. He pushed them up hastily. "Mr. Harker trusts that your wares will be everything they're advertised to be, Ms. Serragno."

Rose stifled a giggle.

Potts left and Marta turned to Rose. "Can you believe that man? When I land this big fish, and I *will*, that worm is going to be one of the first things to go."

"Oh, I don't think he meant anything by it," Rose said, not to reassure Marta so much as to spare Potts his job if she *did* manage to get her hooks into his boss. "Warren Harker's just a busy guy. He trusts us to do a good job, just like we always do."

Marta gave a mild nod. "I'll do a good job, all right. How's that artichoke salad coming along?"

The suite was incredibly posh. Rose had seldom seen such ornate handiwork and she'd worked in some of the finest homes in Manhattan. The chandelier alone must have cost more than a year's worth of her salary. Word was that Harker had two residences in Manhattan, and countless others across the world. Money to burn. Real estate development must be on an upswing.

"Would you care for an hors d'oeuvre?" She asked a group of party guests, holding out the platter with its pretty little assortment of appetizers.

"Oooh! What are those?" a plump, bleached blond woman asked excitedly.

"Avocado egg rolls." One of Rose's better concoctions. "They're particularly good with the tamarind sauce."

The woman drew in her breath appreciatively and took several of them.

"I'll try one of those," a deep voice said behind Rose. Startled, she turned to find herself face-to-face with Warren Harker.

He was taller than she'd realized, even though Marta had gone over his stats quite explicitly. His eyes were a pale, crystal blue, with the faintest laugh lines fanning out into his tanned skin.

"Mr. Harker." She held the platter out to him. "Would you like an hors d'oeuvre?"

"Anything but that artichoke salad your coworker has been chasing me down with." He smiled and picked up a cheese puff.

"You don't like the artichoke salad?"

"I don't like anything held out to me on a spoon with someone saying, 'Come on, just have a little bite.'" He smiled. "Reminds me of my mother trying to get me to eat liver. Not a good memory."

"Oh, I see." Rose groaned inwardly. Marta did have a tendency to be a little heavy-handed when she wanted something. Or, in this case, some*one*. "Look, I'm sorry about that. She's not…" What? Not herself? Marta was being *completely* herself. Not taking her medication? She had a purse full of prescriptions. "She's not usually like that." A lie, but harmless.

"Have you worked with her long?" He had a great voice. Low, smooth, perfectly modulated.

"Just about a year."

"Ever think of striking out on your own?"

She looked at him. "As what?"

"A caterer." He laughed. Very nice laugh. "You *are* the cook in this operation, aren't you?"

Marta didn't like anyone to know that she didn't cook. "One of them."

"One of them," he repeated and gave a broad white smile. "You're good. Loyal. If I were in the food business, I'd try to steal you away right now." At her puzzled look, he explained, "My assistant set this whole thing up, and she says that Serragno never cooks, she just hires the best." He gave a shrug. "Which is why I hired her. And if she hired you, you must be the best. At whatever it is that you do."

Rose gave a wan smile. "I made the artichoke salad."

"Ah." He laughed outright, and several people looked over at them. "I'm sure it tastes far better than this foot I've been chomping on."

Rose couldn't help but chuckle. "If it doesn't, I'm in the wrong business."

"*There* you are." Marta swooped in between them, still holding a ramekin of artichoke salad. She turned to face Warren and took what looked like a deliberate step backward into Rose, loudly knocking the platter to the floor.

Rose's heart sank. All that food, smashed into the carpet.

"Rose Tilden!" Marta snapped. "That was very clumsy. *Look* what you've done to Mr. Harker's carpeting." She turned to Warren with what Rose could only imagine was a look of condescending disgust.

"It wasn't her fault," Warren said, with a slight edge to his voice. "Someone ran into her."

Marta acted as if she hadn't heard him. "Don't worry about a thing, Rose will get that cleaned up." She snaked her arm through his and tried to lead him away. "Why don't you show me your view?"

Warren pulled back and went to Rose. "Let me help you with this," he said, kneeling down in his two-thousand-dollar suit.

"Thanks, but it's not necessary," Rose said quietly.

"No, it isn't." Marta stood over them. "She dropped it, she can pick it up. Now, about that view—"

"Go to any wall," Warren said, helping Rose anyway. "Look out a window. You can't miss it."

Rose felt, rather than saw, Marta's wrath surround them like a cold mist.

"I can get this," she said to him, pulling a mini quiche off the floor. "Please. Go back to your party. I'd feel awful if I kept you from it because of this." And she would be terribly self-conscious if Warren Harker stayed on the floor next to her, picking up bits of food.

"To tell you the truth," he said, his voice quiet, "this is more interesting."

Her face went warm again, and she looked down, hoping he wouldn't notice. "Aren't you enjoying your party?"

"This isn't what I'd call a party," he went on. "It's more of a social obligation. Every summer I have one of these," he nodded at the room, "soirées for the New York bigwigs and corporate head honchos. Got to keep in touch with them, know who's who. I'm in the real estate business, you see."

She was tempted to tell him she knew *all* about him, thanks to Marta, but decided instead to say, "I heard something like that."

He studied her for a moment before continuing. "So this is what you might call good business. Bad party, good business. It happens a lot. I'm sure you see it all the time."

Rose laughed in admission. "You're right. But

most people don't admit they're having a miserable time." She picked up the last fallen appetizer, plopped it on the platter and stood up. "But why bother if you know you're not going to like it?"

He stood up beside her. "See that woman?" He indicated a matronly-looking woman, perhaps in her eighties, dripping with diamonds. The woman had a sour expression on her face, with thin lips, pursed tightly together. "That's Mrs. Winchester, the mayor's mother. Word is, he doesn't make a move without her approval."

"So you need her to approve of you."

"Bingo. So I'm plying her with good food and wine."

"What if she just doesn't like you?"

"She does." He was absolutely confident. "At least for now. She does have her moods, and if she turns against you," he gave a low whistle, "look out."

"She reminds me of a woman I knew when I was a kid. Mrs. Ritter. She owned a flower shop in Brooklyn, which was ironic since she always looked like something smelled funny."

"You're from Brooklyn?"

She nodded. "You?"

He hesitated, then said, "I've spent most of my life right here." He eyed her. "What's your name anyway?"

"Rose. Rose Tilden."

Surprise flickered across his features. "Tilden?"

She nodded.

He frowned. "That's not a name you hear every day."

"I do." She smiled. Almost every day, that is. Since she was two years old. The Barrie Home for Children was on Tilden Street in Brooklyn. All the children who came in without names or identification of any sort were assigned "Tilden." Rose and her sister had come in wearing bracelets that identified their first names but not their last, so they became Rose and Lily Tilden.

"I guess you do," he conceded, but the easy smile he'd worn a few minutes earlier was gone. "Interesting."

"Rose, dear." Marta's voice sounded as if she were two inches behind Rose. "Could you please help Tonya in the kitchen?"

Rose turned to see a look in Marta's eye that she had never seen before. It was sheer anger. "Is something wrong?" Rose asked.

Marta gave a thin-lipped smile. "Certainly not. Tonya simply needs help preparing the dessert tray."

Rose gave Marta a long, hard look, then glanced at Warren and said, "Please excuse me."

He gave a slight nod, then lowered his gaze onto Marta.

Rose didn't see what happened next. She walked to the kitchen resolving with every step to quit this job. She loved the work and really enjoyed most of the people she worked with, but Marta had become more and more of a tyrant lately. Every time a party guest so much as asked Rose if she knew where the ladies' room was, Marta was there, nosing her way in, trying to find out if Rose was being overly familiar with their clients. As if it were a *bad* thing to be cordial in a service-oriented business. What did Marta prefer? That Rose make the "zipping my lips" motion familiar to every third grader in America?

Rose just couldn't deal with her anymore. Serragno might have one of the best reputations in town, but it wasn't the *only* game in town. And Rose would probably be better off working for someone less tempestuous than Marta, even if they weren't as high-profile. Her résumé would survive. She could still have a career.

When she got to the kitchen, Tonya was nowhere to be seen. In fact, the entire room was sparkling clean; there was no food prep out at all. Rose glanced out the opposite doorway and saw that the dessert had already been set up on the table.

"Just what do you think you're doing flirting with the client?" Marta's voice snapped Rose to attention.

"Oh, I'm sorry, that's your job, right?"

"You bet it is." Marta's face went red like the top of a cartoon thermometer. "And I don't want you getting in the middle of my affairs."

"I wasn't flirting with him."

"That's what it looked like to me."

"We were just *talking*."

"I don't pay you to talk, I pay you to cook, serve and clean. That's *all*. Got it? I don't want to catch you doing this again."

"What did you want me to do? Ignore him when he spoke to me?" Rose frowned. "What do you mean *again*?"

"I mean, as you well know, that over these past few months you have gotten bolder and bolder about speaking to our clients. And I don't like it. Every time we do a partly lately, it seems as if you're spending more time chattering with the guests than you are working."

"That is absolutely not true," Rose returned hotly. "I have *never* shirked my duties. As a matter of fact, I defy you to tell me even one time when I didn't do at least fifty percent more than my job description called for." She began untying her Serragno Catering apron. "See? You can't. Because it hasn't happened." She pulled the apron off and folded it. "Look, this isn't working for me and you've made it really obvious it's not working for you, either, so let's just call it a day, okay? Tonya, Keith and the rest of the gang can clean up without me." She put the apron down on the counter. She was so angry her hands were shaking, but she hoped to God that Marta hadn't noticed that.

Marta glanced out the door and then back at Rose. Like melting wax, her facial features relaxed. "Oh, Rose. I'm so sorry. Can you possibly forgive me?"

Rose was taken aback. "What?"

"This has just been so stressful for me." She drew in a shuddering breath and dabbed at her dry eyes. "I just…I've been awful. I know it. I can't blame you for quitting." She gave a humble smile. "I'd do the same thing in your place."

"You would." Something wasn't right here.

Marta nodded. "But the thing is, this is a *very* important party for me. The mayor is out there! He could bring so much business our way. Would you consider staying on at least for the rest of the night?"

"I don't know, Marta…"

"I'll double your pay. Honestly. I'll pay you now. Hand me my purse." She gestured toward a garishly shiny leather purse on a wingback chair in the other room.

"That's not necessary," Rose said, with a sigh. She took the apron off the counter and tied it back on. "I'll finish the night as we agreed. But after that, you're going to have to accept my resignation."

"If you insist." Marta sniffed, then crumpled into a heap on the gleaming tile floor. "Oh, I'm such a mess!" she said in a harsh whisper. "How can I face everyone out there?"

Rose felt completely helpless. What was she supposed to do? "Marta, come on. You'll be fine."

"Could you…could you do one teensy-weensy thing for me?"

Trepidation pounded in Rose's breast. "What's that?"

"Would you get my pill bottle from my purse? The brown one with the yellow lid?"

Rose hesitated for a moment before sighing and saying, "Okay. I'll be right back."

She went to the purse and lifted it. It was heavier than she expected, and one of the first things she touched was a soft clean handkerchief. That was weird. Something didn't compute, but it wasn't until she heard the gasp several feet away that the pieces began to fall into place.

"What are you doing with my purse?"

Rose looked up to see Mrs. Winchester—the mayor's mother—standing with one hand over her mouth and the other pointing at her like a gun.

The noise of the party died down to silence. All eyes turned on Rose.

Suddenly everything moved in slow motion. She turned to see Marta, apparently recovered from her nervous collapse, standing with one hand on her hip and a smug look on her face.

"What's going on?" Warren Harker appeared at the front of the crowd, looking from Mrs. Winchester to Rose. "What's wrong?"

"That—that *girl* was stealing from me!"

"What?" Warren asked sharply, giving Rose a look that could have cut glass.

"Oh, no, no, I wasn't," Rose stammered. "I was just—"

"Put the purse down," Warren said in a cold voice.

Until that moment, she hadn't even realized she was still holding it. She dropped it, as if it were a dead thing, and said, "Marta just asked me to get something from *her* purse and said it was this one." She turned to Marta. "Please. Tell them."

"I cannot believe my eyes," Marta said.

Rose couldn't believe her *ears*. "What?"

When Marta spoke again, Rose knew she'd been set up. "Mr. Harker, I don't know how to apologize enough for this. I don't know what Rose was thinking."

"I was thinking it was your purse, just like you told me," Rose said sharply.

Marta shook her head and clicked her tongue against her teeth. "That's enough, Rose. You've been caught."

It was clear that there was no point in trying to get Marta to tell the truth since she'd gone to considerable trouble to set up the lie.

Instead, Rose turned back to Warren Harker. "Honestly, this is all just a big mistake."

Mrs. Winchester whimpered like a wounded puppy. "I can't believe we're not even safe from theft in a place like this." Her son, the mayor, patted her arm and said to Warren, "This is unacceptable."

"Yes, it is," Warren agreed, eyes on Rose. "I think you'd better go now."

"I will," Rose said, reaching around to untie the apron she had just put back on. "But you have to understand, I was *not* stealing from Mrs. Winchester. I was just trying to get something for Marta from her purse, and she said—"

"Stop!" Marta barked. "You're a liar and I wouldn't blame Mr. Harker for calling the police right now."

"I think you should," Mrs. Winchester agreed, nodding quickly. "Send a message."

Rose's jaw dropped. "This is a mistake!"

"I think you'd better go," Warren said quietly. He moved forward and, with a firm grip on her arm, led her to the front door.

She wrenched her arm free. "You don't need to manhandle me. It's not like I want to stay."

He looked at her for a moment, then shook his head and opened the door. Behind him, she could see the condescending expressions on the faces of his guests. A bunch of wealthy people who were more comfortable believing the "help" would steal than in listening to the truth.

For just a moment when she'd met him, Rose thought maybe Warren was different.

What a foolish mistake that had turned out to be.

One thing was for sure: it was a mistake she would never make again.

Chapter Two

"He sounds like a jerk," Lily pronounced.

"Big-time," Rose agreed. "I don't know if I should conclude never to trust rich guys, or good-looking guys, or both."

Rose and her sister were sprawled on the floor of their Brooklyn apartment, the newspaper Help Wanted section spread around them on the floor.

"How about simply never trusting Warren Harker?" Lily suggested. "Rather than wiping out the entire male population with one fell swoop. Or at least, the entire *desirable* male population."

Rose sighed. "We'll see. Oh, and add Marta Serragno to the list, too. I'm an equal opportunity mistruster."

Lily chuckled. "So she actually used the words, 'You'll never work in this town again'?"

"That's *exactly* what she said." Rose circled another ad in the Help Wanted section of the paper. "And she's as good as her word. So far I've been turned down by every major catering company in the entire city and two of three that are so minor you'd think she wouldn't have ferreted them out."

"Well," Lily said with a straight face, "when you get caught with your hand in the cookie jar, you're going to have to expect repercussions, sis."

"Very funny, Lil. Very, very funny."

"Oh, I'm sorry." Lily threw her arms around Rose and gave her a big squeeze. "I'm just trying to help you see the humor in this. Such as it is. I mean, it's not like you'll *never* work again."

"It's starting to look like it." An ad for a gas station attendant caught Rose's eye and, after a moment of self-pity, she circled it, too.

Lily looked over. "Oh, come on."

"Come on what?"

"You can get a job in the food industry. Gerard said he'd hire you if Miguel didn't already have the job."

Rose mustered a smile. "That's nice of him to say, but since Miguel already *does* have the job, he doesn't really have to put his money where his mouth is." Gerard owned one of the exclusive boutique hotels where Lily worked as a concierge. He'd always been so kind to both of them. "Unless… Maybe he'd hire me as a maid?"

"I'm sure he would, but you'd be miserable."

"I'm miserable now."

"No, I mean you'd be a miserable maid." Lily smiled. "Look at your room. There's hardly a place on the floor where you can see the carpet."

"This is no time to joke, Lily," Rose said, but she smiled.

"Okay, okay. Just trying to add a little levity. Now let's think about this. What if you forget catering for the time being and try restaurants? Maybe even work as a waitress."

"I'd do that gladly. Unfortunately, I've already tried. Same story. Marta Serragno is nothing if not determined. Horrid woman. Half the town seems to be sucking up to her and the other half seems terrified. I can't win."

"Wait a minute." Lily tapped her finger against her chin. "I saw a sign up in one of these places…yes! It was the Cottage Diner. Over by Coney Island?"

"Cottage Diner? I've never heard of it."

Lily shrugged. "It's a greasy spoon, but a great location. Water view and all. The place itself looks like it's been there since World War II. Maybe you could get in there as a waitress and then, you know, work your way up. Put the place on the map. Meantime, I bet the tourists and Coney Island visitors give good tips."

Something in Rose tingled. "That's not a bad idea. There's no way that Marta would have gotten to a crummy little diner in Brooklyn. But if I could help them raise their profile…" She frowned. That was getting ahead of herself. She hadn't even gotten the job—or seen the diner, for that matter—and she was already thinking about raising the place's profile?

As if reading her mind, Lily said, "I'm sure it will work out that way. And I'm telling you, the location is *great*."

"Hmm." For reasons she couldn't quite express— maybe just intuition—this was striking Rose as a good idea. A very good idea. Something told her this could work out in ways she hadn't even thought of. "Where is this place exactly?"

Like the plucky heroine in an old movie, Rose took the Help Wanted sign out of the Cottage Diner window and carried it inside with her to ask for the manager.

She approached a busboy who was clearing dishes from a booth. "Excuse me," she said.

He turned, startled, and dropped a mug onto the floor. It didn't break, but bounced loudly under the booth. He looked at Rose and his face turned red. "Y-yes?"

"I'm here about the job." She indicated the sign she was holding.

If possible, his face turned even more crimson.

"You need to talk to Doc, the owner," a voice barked behind her. "Tim's just a busboy."

She turned to see a craggy-faced customer sitting in another booth, holding a newspaper. There was a steaming cup of coffee in front of him and about ten empty sugar packets. "Doc's in the back." He looked her over skeptically. "But I'm not sure you're exactly what he's looking for. What do you think, Al?"

He looked across the room at the only other customer in the place. The pudgy gray-haired man sneezed, dabbed his nose with a napkin and said, "Give her a break, Dick." He sneezed again and said to Rose, "They've had pretty waitresses here before, but they always leave."

"I'm always willing to try another pretty waitress, though." A bald man in a greasy white apron came out of the kitchen, wiping his hands on a bar towel. "Doc Sears." He set the towel down on the counter and held his hand out.

Rose shook it. "Rose Tilden."

"You're looking for a waitress job?"

"If you're looking for a waitress."

He looked at her skeptically. "You don't look like the kind of waitress we'd get here. Bet you could make a lot of money a few miles into the city."

He was talking about Manhattan, of course. Where she couldn't get so much as a job busing tables. "I live here."

He looked at her as if he wondered what the truth was, but was too tactful to ask. "Can you work evenings?"

She splayed her arms. "Any time you want."

"You gonna stay on longer than a week?"

"I guarantee it."

"Good." He took the sign from her and ripped it in half. "You're hired, Rose Tilden. Can you start tonight?"

Lunchtime had been dead in the diner, and dinner wasn't a whole lot better. Doc was working the grill alongside a short-order cook called Hap, short for Elwood Happersmith. Rose privately concluded that, under the circumstances, she would have preferred Hap, too.

Only about half the booths were full, and the only other waiter was a young man named Paul, who spent more time dozing in an unoccupied booth than waiting tables, leaving Rose to handle pretty much the entire crowd.

She didn't mind, though. She was just glad to have the work.

She was on her feet from two in the afternoon until 10 p.m. With closing time just an hour away, and her feet eagerly awaiting the promise of an Epsom salt bath, her last customer came through the door.

Warren Harker.

She did a double take. If she'd made a list of the

top fifteen people she *least* expected to see in a place like this, Warren Harker would have been close to the top, along with Gandhi and Fidel Castro.

For a moment, she froze, heart pounding. She didn't know if it was the lighting or the fact that she'd spent the day looking at guys like Dick, Al and Doc, but Warren Harker was even more slick-looking than she'd recalled. His dark hair gleamed under the fluorescent lights, his crisp blue suit—with loosened tie and unbuttoned collar—fit like a charm across his wide shoulders.

The jerk.

And now he was her customer. This was spectacularly bad luck. A quick glance at the booth she had already come to think of as "Paul's bed" revealed that the waiter was indeed snoring away, so she was stuck with Warren Harker.

Rose took a quick breath and straightened her back. She could do this. No problem. With a little bit of luck, maybe he wouldn't even remember her.

She walked toward him, feeling a little like a prisoner being led on the final walk down the prison hall. Of all the greasy spoons in all of New York, why why *why* did he have to walk into this one?

"Can I take your order?" she asked, laying on the Brooklyn accent a little thick and keeping her eyes averted.

Her efforts were wasted. Apparently Dick was right in saying they didn't normally have women waiting tables here, because Warren looked up from his paperwork with surprise.

"Hey, you're new," he said.

She barely glanced at him. "Just started today."

He gave a laugh. "Wow, I don't know when I last saw a women working here."

Oh, *no,* he was a regular?

That was it; she was doomed. She was going to lose another job and, given the trouble she had had in finding this one, she didn't know *where* she'd go next.

"So what can I get you?" she asked, keeping her tone short.

"Just a coffee, thanks. And real cream, not milk. Doc's always cheap with the cream."

So he *was* a regular. "Sure thing." She turned to get the coffee, thanking her lucky stars he hadn't realized who she was. Yet.

But she was stopped in her tracks not three feet away.

"Wait a minute."

She closed her eyes, dreading what was coming next.

"I know you, don't I?"

She could feel his eyes on her back, sending a tickle straight down her spine.

"Don't think so," she answered without turning around.

"Come here." It was practically a command. Apparently he was so used to having people jump when he told them to that he felt perfectly comfortable bossing everyone around.

She took the coffee carafe from the counter and turned to go back to his table. She kept her eyes downcast, in the ridiculous hope that if she didn't look at him, he wouldn't see her. Ostrich logic. "What is it?"

"I know we've met."

She shook her head. "Don't think so." Then she made the mistake of glancing at him.

His blue eyes looked her over for a moment before he snapped his fingers. "Serragno Catering."

"I—"

"You're Rose Tilden!"

Chapter Three

"What the hell are you doing *here?*" he went on, before she'd even had a moment to respond.

His tone was so sharp, so downright *accusatory,* that she was taken aback. "I'm working here."

"What?" He looked around, as if trying to find confirmation that this was true.

"I'm working here."

"That's impossible."

She tightened her grip on the coffee carafe, tempted to assure him that his wallet was safe from her. But she bit her tongue and instead tried to be mindful of her job. "Do you need more sugar?"

He looked at her for a long moment, before shaking his head. "I don't do sugar."

You don't do sweet, either, she thought pouring coffee into his cup. "Well, is there anything else I can get you? We're closing up soon."

"Nothing," he said, distracted. "How long have you been working here?"

"Are you investigating me, Mr. Harker?"

"Should I be?"

Good lord, he sounded serious! "Of course not!" she responded quickly. "I was joking."

"That's reassuring." His tone remained even. Cool.

Accusatory.

"Mr. Harker, are you implying something? If so, I really wish you'd come right out and say it."

"Hey, now, what's going on here?" Doc came out of the kitchen and ambled over to the booth. "You two know each other?"

"We've met," Warren said, keeping his eyes on Rose.

Her heart pounded as she wondered what else he would say to Doc and if she would lose her job because of it. For a moment, she stood there, suspended in time, filled with anxiety at the thought of what Warren might reveal.

Then she decided she would just tell Doc the truth herself. There was no point in standing around wondering if someone else was going to control her future; she had to do it herself.

"I worked for a caterer at one of Mr. Harker's

parties," she said to Doc. "I was falsely accused of stealing and lost my job because of it, but I promise you I didn't do it."

Doc laughed and patted Rose's arm. "You're as wound up as an old alarm clock, aren't you? I know you wouldn't steal anything."

Her shoulders slumped in relief. "Thank you."

"What sort of idiot accused you of stealing?"

She glanced uneasily at Warren.

"No!" Doc exclaimed. "Not you!"

Warren gave a small shrug. "The evidence was, as they say, overwhelming."

Doc looked at Warren incredulously. "What are you, crazy?"

"I've been called worse than that," Warren said. Then he frowned and added, "I think I've even been called worse than that by you, Doc."

Doc furrowed his brow. "Then you deserved it, I'm sure. Now it sounds like this little lady has been through enough. You ease up, Harker, or you'll find yourself drinking some mighty cold coffee in here."

Warren took his wallet out, opened it and left a twenty on the table for the dollar fifty check. "Your coffee isn't that good to begin with, Doc."

"Hmmph." Doc crossed his arms in front of his barrel chest. "You drink too much of it anyway."

Warren laughed, then headed for the door without looking back at Rose. "See you next time."

"Be nice to my waitress," Doc called after him, then turned back to Rose. "See? He's not so bad."

"Maybe," she said doubtfully, watching the dashing figure of Warren Harker walk out the door and into the night. "Does he come in here very often?"

"Few times a week. He's been in quite a lot lately."

Her heart sank. This was going to be trouble for her. "Why? He doesn't live near here."

"Nah. Just likes to hang out here, I guess." Doc gave her an encouraging smile. "Don't worry about him. He may be a big shot up in the city, but around here he's just another fella looking for a cup of coffee. Now let's wake Paul up and get out of here. Got another day of work tomorrow, you know."

Warren Harker leaned back against the leather seats of his Town Car and watched the drizzly gray city pass by. It had been unseasonably cold and rainy all day, and his mood had grown worse by the hour, along with the weather.

Now, on what promised to be a long wait in traffic on the drive to Brooklyn, he sat back and tried to figure out what was troubling him so much.

It came to him in two words: Rose Tilden.

For two days, he hadn't been able to get her off his mind.

What was she up to? What was she doing at the Cottage, of all places? There was no way it was just a coincidence and although Warren didn't like to draw the worst conclusion, it was inevitable. She had to be some sort of corporate spy. Some clever and strange variation on the theme—a cross between Mata Hari and Donald Trump. He had heard rumblings that something like that was going on, but at first he had dismissed it as rumors. Now he wasn't so sure.

If her contact with him had just ended with the caterer, he never would have suspected a thing. Whoever had sent her, if indeed someone had, had been smart to take that route. If he were a less honest businessman, he'd be jotting it down in his notes for future reference.

But once she showed up at the Cottage…well, that was bad planning. It was just too specific to be chance, wasn't it? Of all the tiny, obscure little places she might have gotten a job, why the Cottage? He couldn't even remember the last time he'd seen a woman working there. Maybe never. It was in what was generally regarded as a slightly unsavory part of town. That was one of the reasons he was spending so much time there. In fact, the neighborhood was still a diamond in the rough. He could buy property for a song and turn it around in no time.

Which was exactly what he intended to do.

He could think of three adversaries right off the top of his head who would have paid big money to find out what and where he was planning to develop next.

Had Rose figured it out? The real reason he was spending so much time in that booth at the Cottage was that he was planning to buy the building opposite it just as soon as he could get the owner—a creaky old man who ran a dry cleaner on the ground floor that never seemed to have customers—to sell.

Warren couldn't figure out why he wouldn't accept any of his offers, though there were rumors of money laundering and vague Mob ties, so he had to keep an eye on the place to watch for changes. As soon as the old guy relented, and surely he would eventually, Warren had to pounce.

Then he'd tear the building down and use the space to build one of his luxury apartment complexes. More and more people were moving out of the heart of the city, for more and more reasons. Now was the time to bring the Harker touch to the suburbs of Manhattan.

Unless, of course, Monroe Associates or Chuck Donohue or Apex got wind of his plans and sabotaged them somehow.

The question was, who among them would go so far as to hire a beautiful woman to spy on him?

And had she figured out anything about his plans yet?

Rose's first two weeks of work flew by. She liked being busy. And the truth was, she was enjoying working in her old hometown, a stone's throw from the nostalgic beauty of Coney Island. It was still hot for mid-October, and there were a lot of tourists who kept the place hopping.

Toward the end of her night shift one Thursday night, it occurred to her that Warren Harker hadn't been in for days. That led to a long series of troubling thoughts about the man; mostly troubling because once she started thinking about him she couldn't *stop*.

"What's on your mind, Miss Rose?" the busboy, Stu, asked. "You look sad."

She sat down at the counter, glad to take a load off her aching feet. "Stu, do you know Warren Harker?"

He pressed his lips together and looked up and to the left, as if trying to see something very far away. "Mmm…I don't think so."

"Yeah you do," Paul said with a yawn as he passed by with some plates in his hand. "Mr. Harker."

Realization lit Stu's eyes. "Oh, yeah, Mr. Harker. Sure. He's in here all the time."

Rose tried to keep from smiling. Stu was just like a child. It was going to take a while to get used to it. "Has he been here a lot?"

"Sure," Paul said, clattering the dishes into the sink and turning back to her. "Few times a week. Always sits in that same booth." He pointed to where Warren had, indeed, been sitting the last time she saw him.

"Why does he come *here* do you think?"

"Best food in Brooklyn," Stu said.

"Horse manure," Dick called from his booth several yards away. "If this is the best food in Brooklyn, Brooklyn is in trouble."

At this point the short-order cook, Hap, poked his head out of the window from the kitchen. "Then why are you in here all the time, you big lug?" he asked with a bright, red-faced smile.

Dick gave a grumpy shrug and turned his eyes back to the racing section of the newspaper. "Close to home."

Hap chuckled. "Customer's a customer, I guess. No matter why they come in."

"So why do *you* think Warren Harker comes in here?" Rose asked him. "I mean, the guy's as rich as Croesus. He could eat anywhere. He could hire an entire cooking staff to be on call twenty-four hours. Why come to a little place like this, no matter how good the food is?"

"You think he doesn't like the food here?" Stu asked, frowning.

"No, I'm not saying that. I'm just wondering if there's some other reason he comes here." Not that she could think of one. If he hadn't been coming all along, she'd have worried that he was so angry about what happened at his party that he came here to get her fired, but she knew no one was that petty. No one except Marta.

Still, it just didn't make sense that he came *here*. It was just so far from his world. And now that he hadn't been for a few days, she wondered if he'd stopped coming because of her, because he didn't trust her.

"Who are you talking about?" someone asked behind her.

Thinking it was Al, she turned, saying, "Warren Ha—" She stopped mid-word, shocked to say the man himself standing in front of her. "Warren Harker, what a pleasant surprise," she fudged.

He gave a nod. "Nice recovery. Now, you want to tell me why you're asking about me, or should I tell you what I think?"

This time it was Doc who poked his head out of the kitchen. "Hey, now, Harker, I don't want any trouble from you. I've already told you to leave the poor girl alone."

"It's okay," Rose told him.

Warren raised his eyebrows. "Join me for a moment?"

She glanced back at the worried faces of her coworkers, and gave a reassuring smile that felt more as if she were gritting her teeth. "Sure," she said to Warren, following him to the booth.

He sat down and indicated she should do the same, but she shook her head. "I'll stand, thanks." She realized, then, that she had the carafe of coffee in her hand. It made for an awkward prop, but it was too late for her to go back and put it away now, so she poured some into the cup on his table.

Warren leveled his cool blue eyes on her. "So you want to know why I come here to the Cottage."

"I was curious about it, yes."

"What I want to know is why you're curious about it." He narrowed his eyes and lowered his voice.

She didn't have a quick answer to that. She was curious because she was curious. There wasn't a lot more to it than that. But the way Warren was looking at her, one would have thought it was positively *sinister* of her.

"What are you really up to?" he asked her in a low tone.

"What am I *up* to? Nothing! What are you suggesting?"

"You tell me."

"Is this about what happened at your party?" She did *not* like being accused of anything she hadn't done, and she definitely didn't like to have to keep on defending herself. "If so, you've got it all wrong. You *did* hire a dishonest caterer, but it wasn't me. Marta Serragno had her eye on you before she even got to your suite, and when I made the foolish mistake of talking to you, she got jealous and set me up. It's that simple."

"Why would she do that?" he asked, nonplussed. "It doesn't make her business look good if she hires thieves."

Rose winced at the designation of *thief.* "I think it was a rather impromptu decision on her part. Maybe she figured it was the lesser of two evils. I don't know." She threw her hands in the air. "Actually, you know what? I don't care. If you want to believe a black widow like Marta Serragno, more power to you. It's not my problem."

He leaned back and let out a long breath. "Okay, let's be honest. I think you know I'm not concerned about what happened at my party."

"You're not?"

He shook his head. "Not at the moment. At the moment, I'm more concerned with what you were doing there in the first place. And what you're doing here now. Tell me the truth, Ms. Tilden, and I'll go easy on you. Has someone hired you to watch me?"

Now *that* was definitely not expected. "Has someone hired me to *watch* you?" she repeated incredulously.

He gave a short nod. "I'll double what they're paying you if you tell me who it is."

She didn't know whether to be amused or insulted. Or just plain flummoxed. "Why on earth would someone want me—or anyone—to watch you? Are you doing something that needs to be watched?"

He gave a quick shake of his head. "Nothing at all. But I do a lot of business in this city. Not everyone wishes me well."

"And you think they hire *spies?*" She gave a laugh. "To watch you eat? I don't see how that helps anyone who has it in for you. Unless, of course, they hired me to lace your coffee with arsenic."

He raised an eyebrow.

"No one did." She shook her head. "But the way you treat people, I wouldn't be at all surprised if someone wanted to do just that."

He watched her through narrowed eyes. "I find it quite a coincidence that you worked for the caterer in my suite and now, suddenly, you're working here."

"It's not a coincidence at all," she said simply.

"No?"

"No. I'm working here because I was falsely accused of a crime by your caterer, and this was the only place that would hire me. Now I'd appreciate it if you could stop insinuating things about my character, lest I should lose *another* job because of you."

"I'm not trying to get you fired."

"Good. I'm glad to hear it. Now, if you're satisfied that I'm not spying on you or going to pick your pocket, how about we pretend we've never met?"

"Fine."

"Good. Do you want anything else with your coffee?"

He shook his head. "But keep it coming. It could be a long night."

Chapter Four

Damn it. What now?

Warren drank his coffee slowly, watching Rose move about the restaurant, waiting tables and carrying dirty plates back to the kitchen every time young Stu forgot to do it himself.

She really was quite a sight. Curvy and luscious in her pink-and-white waitress uniform, she looked like something out of a 1950s' Coca-Cola advertisement. With her long chestnut hair pulled back into a thick ponytail and her red bee-stung lips and wide green eyes, she looked the picture of the all-American girl next door.

Could he really have been so wrong about her?

He had to find out. He hated to waste George

Smith's ace investigation skills on something like this, something arguably *personal*, but he didn't have any choice. If someone had hired her to watch him, it could affect his business. If not, well, he owed her an apology.

But, man, he hated apologizing.

He took his cell phone out and dialed George's number. The investigator answered on the first ring.

"Smith."

"It's Harker," Warren said, watching Rose across the room. The guy with the blond hair who was always sneezing, Al, said something and they both laughed.

She had a nice laugh. Robust and unself-conscious.

"I have something I need you to do for me," Warren said quietly into the phone. Rose laughed again and he added, "As soon as possible."

Six days later, George Smith was sitting in front of Warren in his Manhattan office.

"The chick's as clean as a whistle," George pronounced, setting a thin folder down on Warren's desk. "As far as I can tell, she's never even had an overdue library book."

"What about her family? Her name, Tilden—"

"It's just as you suspected. From age two, she grew up in the Barrie Home along with a sister named Lily. She lives with the sister now in a small place on the south side of town. There was another sister who was adopted soon after they were taken into the home. Laurel Standish. Last known to work as a nurse somewhere upstate, but she's not there anymore. Do you need me to dig up more on her?"

"Is she close to Rose or the other sister?"

"Lily." George shook his head. "Not at all. They don't seem to have had any contact at all for years."

"Then let's not worry about her right now." Warren picked up the folder and leafed through the pages as George spoke.

"The rest is there. She went to the local schools, same ones you went to, I believe. And she graduated from high school with honors. No college. Went to culinary school for a short time." George shrugged. "I see absolutely nothing to suggest she has personal contact with anyone you're concerned about, much less an inclination to work for them."

"Not the corporate espionage type, huh?"

"Not at all."

"Which, in my book, makes her a good candidate."

George smiled. "I thought you'd say that. So I tailed her. All week. You'll see that in my bill."

Warren flipped a page and saw George's hourly log. "That's a lot of hours."

"Hey, you want peace of mind?"

Warren set the folder down. "Go on."

"Nothin'. Zip. She goes to work, she goes home, cooks, watches some TV, sleeps. Talks to her sister. A couple of times, they had friends over for drinks and food, but no one of interest. I checked 'em all out. Frankly, the girl's about as ordinary as they come."

"She's not ordinary," Warren said, picturing her bustling around the diner. "She's far from ordinary."

"Lifestylewise, she's ordinary." George chuckled. "You're not paying me to draw conclusions about her sexy little sashay or the ways in which she could drive a man crazy."

"No, I'm not," Warren said coolly, giving George a warning glance. "Remember that."

George's face went pink and he cleared his throat uncomfortably. "All right, then, I think that's pretty much it. There weren't even any phone conversations to speak of."

"You tapped her phone?"

"You paid me to investigate her."

Warren nodded and gave a shrug. That might have been crossing a line, given that Rose was innocent of any wrongdoing, but there was nothing he could do about it now. Except, of course, not ask about it. "And what did you hear?"

"Nothing unusual. Calls with friends, making plans to meet. That sort of thing."

"Any…any men?" Warren shifted in his chair and tried to assume a nonchalant facial expression, as if he were just idly curious.

The look George gave him left no doubt but that he was on to him. "Not for almost a year." He nodded toward the folder. "Like I said, it's all in there."

"Okay, thanks, George." Warren stood up and put his hand out. "Great job, as always."

George shook his hand and nodded. "One more thing."

"Yeah?"

"The old man who owns the dry cleaner over in Brooklyn? Pinkney? He died last week. His son's running the place now."

Warren nodded thoughtfully. Now it was time to make his move. "Thanks a lot, George."

George smiled. "Let me know if you need anything else."

"I will," Warren said, sitting back down, the folder still in hand. "I will."

When George had gone, Warren picked up the phone and called his lawyer, Mark Benning. "The owner died yesterday. His son's there now. Make an offer."

"I'm on it."

"And Benning?"

"What?"

"Let's not waste a lot of time with this. Make it an offer he can't refuse." He hung up the phone and winced at the unintentional *Godfather* line he'd spouted. It was appropriate in a way, though, if what he'd heard about Pinkney was correct.

Benning called back less than an hour later. "He won't give up the building."

"*What?* How much did you offer him?"

Benning quoted the figure that had been the most Warren had been willing to risk. He was astonished. "What the hell is going on there?"

"I think the rumors must be true."

"I guess so."

"Want me to make another offer?"

"Yes." Warren nodded his head, even though the man on the phone couldn't see him. "Do whatever it takes."

The Cottage was closing in fifteen minutes on Thursday night when Warren Harker came in. It had been quite a night. The police had swarmed the building across the street right before the dinner hour and people had swarmed into the diner to watch the activity.

No one knew what was going on, though a lot of people seemed to think it had something to do with the Mafia. Eventually the police had left without taking anyone into custody, and old Dick had commented about "those guys" being "made of Teflon."

Warren Harker came in just as they were wrapping things up for the night.

"Coffee?" she asked him as she set down utensils on a booth for breakfast the next morning.

"Sure," he said. "And if you can spare a few minutes, I'd like to talk to you."

It had been a long day and she wasn't up for more accusations, but at the same time it was hard to say no to him. Lily would have told her it was because of his dark-haired, blue-eyed good looks, but in reality she figured it was probably just because she was polite. It seemed rude to say no.

She looked around for an excuse in the form of a customer, but there was no one there, so she had little choice but to join him.

"Let me tell you up front that I'm not interested in any more of your crazy accusations," she told him. "And I need this job pretty badly, so I'd really appreciate it if you didn't stir up any ill feelings toward—"

"I want to apologize."

For a moment, she thought she might have misheard him. "You want to *what?*"

"You heard me."

"I'm not sure I did."

He groaned and raked his hand through his hair. "Look, I realize I might have been wrong about you."

"*Might* have been?"

"Maybe." He flattened his hand and tipped it side to side. "I'm willing to give you the benefit of the doubt."

"That's gracious of you." Her green eyes danced as she looked at him.

They were interrupted by Doc. "I'm cutting out a little early," he said. "The wife wants to have a late dinner to celebrate our anniversary. Can you lock up, Rosie?"

"Sure. Happy anniversary. How long has it been?"

He gave a good-natured smile. "Longer than any man has a right to hope for. Fifty-two years."

"Congratulations," Warren said. "Esther deserves a medal."

Doc laughed. "Don't think she doesn't know it!"

Rose was surprised Warren knew Doc's wife's name. She hadn't realized he was actually friends with the old fellow. Maybe Warren wasn't quite as detached as he appeared to be.

Doc left and Rose turned to Warren. "You heard the man. I have to lock up."

Warren stood up. "I'll wait and give you a ride."

She gave a dry laugh. "I think I can handle it myself."

His face remained serious. "All the same, I'd feel better if you let me give you a ride home."

She thought of the police activity earlier. But they hadn't found anything. They'd left, so surely that meant everything was okay out there. In a way, she'd rather take her chances with Brooklyn than with Warren. "It's not necessary," she said. "I live just a few blocks away."

"You live seven blocks away, and that's a long walk this time of night."

"How do you know where I live?"

Her question seemed to catch him off guard, as if it made him realize that he'd said more than he'd intended. "I don't."

"You said I live seven blocks away and I do."

"Oh. Well. It's just that there's no housing for at least three blocks from here. I just said seven. Could have said eleven or eight, or whatever."

She frowned. Maybe that had been all he'd meant. But she *did* live seven blocks away. *Exactly* seven blocks away.

"Honest," he said. "I've never even seen your house."

"It's an apartment."

"There, see? It was just a lucky guess. Now let me give you a ride since we've established that your abode, whatever it is, isn't very far away."

She shook her head thoughtfully. "Thanks for the offer, but I'd rather just go home myself."

He shrugged. "Suit yourself." He headed for the door and she followed. They both stepped into the mild night air and he waited while she turned and locked the door.

When she was through, she turned back to him and said, pointedly, "Good night."

"Good night," he said, but he didn't move. A sleek black Town Car moved to the curb, as quiet as a cat in the dark.

Rose stepped behind the car and crossed the street. There was no one on the road, so she ran across and was about to turn west toward home when she noticed something lying on the sidewalk several yards in the opposite direction.

Something large.

Or, rather, some*one* large.

She glanced nervously back across the street. Warren Harker was getting into the car. He wasn't looking in her direction or she could have caught his attention. For a moment, she thought to call out to him, but on second thought she didn't want to get all worked up over what might actually end up being nothing.

Biting her lower lip, she looked back toward the thing on the sidewalk. Maybe it was just a bag of clothes from the dry cleaner. That was probably it.

She walked toward it, telling herself it was just clothes but that she had to check it out just in case.

As she got closer, though, she knew it wasn't just clothes.

The thing lying on the sidewalk, with what Rose could now see was a trickle of blood staining the white concrete next to it, was Doc.

Chapter Five

Warren had just instructed his driver to turn around and follow Rose home at a subtle distance when he heard her scream.

"Stop the car!" He didn't even wait for it to come to a complete halt; he just sprang from the moving vehicle and ran to where Rose was standing.

"What's wrong?"

"It's Doc!" Rose pointed at something lying on the sidewalk in a heap. "He's been hurt." She bent down to him.

"Don't move him," Warren instructed, taking his cell phone out of his pocket. He dialed 911, gave their location, then flipped the phone closed and went to Doc.

He was a mess. Out cold, and there was a nasty gash on his head sending a river of blood onto the sidewalk next to him. His leg was bent under him at an awkward angle. His pulse was weak, but at least there *was* a pulse. That meant it wasn't too late.

Yet.

Rose was patting Doc gently on his chest. "It's okay, Doc," she said softly, her voice soothing. "Help's on the way. You're going to be fine." But the quiver in her voice betrayed the fact that she was terrified he *wouldn't* be fine.

"Do you have any idea what happened?" Warren asked.

She shook her head, still focusing her attention on the older man. "I just found him like this." She looked at Warren with wide eyes. "He left at least fifteen minutes ago. He must have been here all this time. And that's a lot of blood." Her voice caught in her throat, but she didn't break down and cry.

"Head wounds always bleed a lot," Warren reassured her. "It might not be as bad as it looks."

"It looks bad all right," she said, taking Doc's limp hand in hers. "It just looks so bad."

Warren watched her tenderness toward Doc and knew, all at once, that there was no way Rose Tilden was anything other than what she seemed. A good woman with a good heart. He'd misjudged her, then given her a snide apology. She deserved better treatment than that.

When this was over, he was going to do something—he wasn't yet sure what—to make it up to her. Maybe he'd buy a restaurant and hire her as the executive chef. Not that he knew anything about restaurants, but it couldn't be *that* different from any other business venture.

But none of that mattered right now. All that mattered right now was Doc.

Sirens sounded in the distance and within a couple of minutes, an ambulance rounded the corner on screeching wheels and pulled up to the curb. The paramedics got out and within seconds were taking Doc's vital signs. After pronouncing him stable, at least for the moment, they put him onto a stretcher and lifted him into the ambulance.

Rose watched, kneading her hands in front of her. Every once in a while she told them to "be gentle" or "easy." Her posture was ramrod stiff until they finally closed the ambulance doors and headed for Coney Island Hospital.

It was only when the ambulance had gone and the street was quiet again that Rose cried. She put her hands to her face and sobbed silently into them, her shoulders shaking convulsively.

"Hey." Warren was at a loss. He'd never been good with emotional women, but he couldn't just stand there and let her cry. "He'll be all right," he said, putting a hand gingerly upon her shoulder. "I'm sure he will. He's a tough old dog."

"He was just lying here in the dark and cold, all alone." She sniffed. "What if he'd died?"

"He didn't."

"But—"

"It's not worth thinking about," Warren told her firmly. "He's going to be fine." He rested his hand on her shoulder. It was warm and soft, and he would have taken her into his arms except he was afraid the gesture would be misconstrued. "Doc was a war hero, you know. He's been through far worse things than this."

"He's not a young soldier anymore."

"No," Warren said, looking her in the eye. "He's an old soldier now. And there's nothing tougher than an old soldier."

She looked back at him, and gave a shaky smile. "I hope you're right."

"I am." He hoped. "Now, you don't happen to know Doc's home phone number, do you?"

"Oh, my God, his wife must be frantic! We've got to call her."

"That's what I'm planning to do. Do you know the number?"

She shook her head. "But he lives on Gooding."

Warren took out his cell phone and asked information for Doc's number. He broke the news to Esther, who was so alarmed that Rose could probably hear her several feet away. Warren did his best to reassure Esther, and he told her he'd meet her in the hospital waiting room in fifteen minutes. After that, he called a local cab company and had a car sent to pick Esther up.

"That was nice of you," Rose said to him when he hung up. "She's lucky you were here. We all were."

He shrugged that off. "Come on, let me give you a ride home on my way to the hospital."

She shook her head. "No, I want to go to the hospital, too. I have to make sure Doc's okay."

"It's going to be a long night."

"I don't care. I'm going."

It was obvious that Rose wasn't a woman who could be told what to do.

It was equally obvious that she was a woman who didn't change her mind very easily once she'd made it up.

Which made it completely obvious that there was no point in Warren objecting.

"Okay." He gestured toward the car. "Let's go."

It was a long wait.

There was talk of minor surgery, tens of stitches and dilating pupils. The news alternated between being frightening and encouraging, and the roller-coaster ride, combined with coffee, had Warren's adrenaline pumping.

Around 2 a.m., Esther was finally allowed in to see Doc. Shortly after that, she came out and told Rose and Warren he wanted to see them.

He was propped up in bed. The wound on his head had been cleaned and stitched so extensively it looked like something Dr. Frankenstein had put together, and his entire left leg was in a hard cast. His face was drawn and pale.

"Thanks for sticking around with Esther tonight," Doc said weakly. "You two are real friends."

Warren's chest tightened. It was hard to see the old guy so weak. He'd known him for thirty-odd years and in that time he'd always been the same robust character who ran the diner day to day. Now, for the first time, Warren could see how old Doc really was.

"Es, honey, would you see if you can get me some ice chips?" Doc asked his wife.

"Sure I will," she answered with the thick Brooklyn accent that had always made Warren smile. "Where's that nurse?" She bustled out into the hall.

Warren knew that Doc had been trying to get Esther out of the room for a moment for some reason, but nothing could have prepared him for what Doc would say next.

"The guy who did this to me," Doc said, his eyes focused on Warren, "he had a message for you."

"For *me?*" Suddenly Warren could feel Rose's eyes on him. "What do you mean? What message?"

Doc glanced at Rose. "I don't want you to hear this but I think you have to. You might not want to work at the diner any more once you do, and I wouldn't blame you one bit."

"I'm not going to quit on you," she reassured him, putting a hand softly on his forearm.

"What was the message?" Warren asked a little impatiently.

Doc turned watery blue eyes back to him. "That you'd better stay out of the neighborhood. To cancel your plans."

"Me?"

"You. He said Warren Harker."

"What are your plans?" Rose asked him, alarmed. "Are you involved with the people who did this to Doc?"

"Of course not," he said.

"Then why did they give Doc a message for you right before they did this to him?"

"I don't know, but I'm sure as hell going to find out."

"I hope you do it before someone else gets hurt."

He was desperate for her to stop talking so as not to alarm Doc any more than he already was. "No one else is going to get hurt," he said through his teeth.

"How do you know? You just said you have no idea why this happened!"

"I told you I'm going to find out," he said. "Now drop it."

"Now, now," Doc said from his hospital bed. "Calm down, you two."

Warren was immediately sorry. He had no right to stress Doc out any more than he already was. "It sounds," he said, a little more patiently, "like typical gang stuff. They saw me hanging around and are afraid I'm going to turn their few blocks of lawless neighborhood into a development." Which was exactly what he was going to do.

"This was no little street gang," Doc said to Warren meaningfully. "These guys mean business."

Warren understood. "I'm not afraid of them."

"Good. But make sure no one else gets hurt in the cross fire." He jerked his head toward Rose.

"Don't worry about anyone but yourself," she said to Doc. "You need to get well. Now, what can we do to help you?"

"Glad you asked. As a matter of fact, I do need your help. Both of you."

"Anything," Warren said, and meant it.

"You name it," Rose said.

"I'm not going to be able to cook for a while." He looked at his leg and gave a single dry chuckle. "No cracks about me never being able to, Harker."

Warren smiled.

Doc continued, "Rosie, you told me you came from a cooking background. Think you could handle the kitchen at the diner?"

"I'd be glad to try, but what about Hap?"

Doc shook his head. "Hap's good at doing what he's told. Peel ten pounds of potatoes, he's your man. But he's no cook."

"Okay." Rose smiled at him. "You've got it."

"Thank you." He turned his attention to Warren. "I need your help, too. It's important."

"Tell me what you need."

Doc let out a long breath. "I've had the Cottage for more than fifty years. My parents had it before that. In that time, no more than two days have passed without a family member running it. Until now, that is." He sighed heavily. "The doctors say I can't go back to work for several weeks." He gestured toward his cast leg. "Even then, it's going to be hard to get around. Anyway, there are very few people I'd trust to keep the business running." His eyes met Warren's. "But I trust you."

"Absolutely," Warren said. "I'll get someone on it right away. I'll have the best restaurant manager in the business there by the end of the day tomorrow."

Doc put up a hand. "I don't want someone I don't know poking around my place. I want *you* there."

Warren hesitated. He was in charge of a real estate empire. He didn't have time to spend twelve hours a day in a diner that was worth less than some of his cars!

He was about to voice that, when he looked at the old man and saw that the value of this wasn't in the real estate or the building itself. The value was in the generations of family that were behind it. The pride Doc took in keeping the business running, even when there was a new fast-food restaurant around every corner. Doc didn't understand Warren's business, and it didn't matter. He trusted Warren to be a friend at this time.

On top of that, it was Warren's fault Doc was even in this predicament.

"I'll do it," Warren said. "Anything. For as long as you need me to. You can count on me."

Rose got home at 3:30 a.m. She and Warren had agreed they should get what sleep they could and assess what needed to be done at the diner after hours that night. She told him she'd run it for the day and let the other employees know what had happened, so that Warren could take the time to go to his office in Manhattan and get a few things done.

"Will Doc be okay?" Stu asked her anxiously at least ten times during the day.

Each time, she assured him, "Yes, he'll be back before you know it."

Even Paul managed to wake up and wait tables while Rose took over the back kitchen duties. Hap was, just as Doc had said, an excellent prep worker, but he didn't have a clue how Doc made the chili or chicken noodle soup, or anything that had more than three ingredients and didn't go on the grill.

So Rose decided she'd have to wing it. She'd make the same dishes that were on the menu, but since Doc hadn't written down any recipes, she'd just use her own.

During a lull in the dinner hour, she called Doc's

suppliers and ordered meat and vegetables to be delivered at dawn. She had some long days ahead of her, but she was determined to do her absolute best to keep Doc's business running smoothly. She didn't know how long he'd be out of commission, but it didn't take long for restaurants to go under if they lost enough business, and she wasn't about to let that happen.

Neither was Warren.

He arrived close to 8 p.m. and took out all of Doc's financial books from an unlocked safe in the back. He spread them out on one of the booths and pored over them.

By 10 p.m., he realized the Cottage was bankrupt.

"What are you talking about?" Rose asked. "How can it be bankrupt? He's paid all of us on time every week. Customers are coming in. I placed two large orders with suppliers today on his accounts and they didn't say it was a problem."

Warren frowned. "You ordered things today?"

She nodded. "I *had* to. We were completely out of beef for chili and the one carrot left in the refrigerator didn't even snap when I broke it in half." She shuddered at the memory.

He moved some papers around, took out the bank statement and asked, "Can I see your orders?"

She shrugged. "I don't have the invoices yet, obviously, but I've got my own lists." She went to the counter and gathered the papers containing her lists.

He took the sheets when she handed them to him. "Prime beef," he read. "Couldn't you just use the cheaper stuff?"

The quick answer was no, but she knew he wouldn't accept that. "If you feed people food made from subpar ingredients once, you'll get paid for one meal and they won't come back. Use the best and they'll come back again and again."

"Nice theory," Warren said shortly. "But I don't see anything here to justify the extra expenditure. Did you check Doc's previous invoices to see what he normally buys?"

"No," she confessed. "Since he didn't leave any recipes, I figured I'd have to use my own, so I ordered what I knew I'd need." She didn't add that she suspected he probably usually got the cheaper stuff and that could account, at least partially, for the quality of his food.

"Organic carrots," Warren read off the list, then raised an eyebrow in her direction. *"Organic?"*

She sat up straight, ready to defend her position. "They taste better and, frankly, I think they're better for you."

"They also cost almost twice as much as conventional."

"Well, they're twice as good." Her face felt warm. She knew what he was getting at. He thought she'd been a spendthrift with someone else's account. He didn't understand that she had the opportunity to grab the late-season tourist trade and make the Cottage into a destination restaurant as well as a neighborhood diner. Yes, Doc's business was down. But she'd heard enough complaints about the food to know why. After his impassioned plea at the hospital to keep his family business alive, she knew she had to do whatever she could to help fix it.

"Cancel the orders," Warren said, dropping the papers. "All of them."

"What?"

"You heard me. Cancel the orders. Better still, give me the numbers. I'll do it."

"You're not a cook!"

"And you are clearly not a financier." He leaned back in the booth and looked at her wearily. "Doc can't afford your order."

"He'll be able to in a few days," she said. "I'm sure of it."

"What if you're wrong?" There was a challenge in his cool blue eyes.

She shot the challenge right back at him. "I'm not."

"I don't like the odds."

"You can't even read the odds. You have no idea how the restaurant business works."

"From what I can see, it doesn't."

She sighed. "But you *know* that's not true. Even this place has been here for fifty-odd years. Maybe longer. Sometimes you have to put out a little money in order to *make* money." She shrugged. "You've got to play to win."

He looked at her evenly. "When did you place the orders?"

"Earlier this afternoon."

"It's too late to cancel, isn't it?"

She hesitated, then admitted, "Yes. But that's not the reason I'm sticking to my guns on this."

He shook his head. "I'll cover this order myself, then. Just don't tell Doc. He'd hate that."

"You don't need to cover it. I'm telling you, with Veterans Day this week and the mild weather bringing tourists in, we'll get enough business to pay the account by the end of the week."

"If it weren't Doc's business at stake, I'd almost be satisfied to prove you wrong, but we'd need to feed the entire population of China in order to bring this place into the black this week."

What an arrogant jerk! She realized that was the very character trait that had probably gotten him as far as he'd gone, but that didn't make her like him. "If it weren't Doc's business at stake," she told him coolly, "I wouldn't be working my tail off for what will probably end up being *considerably* less than the minimum hourly wage."

He gave a dry laugh. "Keep spending the way you are, and you'll be lucky to get that."

She stood up, untying her apron angrily as she spoke. "You do your job, Mr. Harker, and I'll do mine. I can assure you that if the diner doesn't maintain or increase business over the next few weeks, it won't be because of me."

"You're right, because I'm placing the orders from now on."

She tossed the apron over onto the counter and turned to him, hands on hips. "Really? How many pounds of strawberries do you need to order for two days' worth of strawberry shortcake?"

"I'll find out."

"Really? Where?"

He splayed his arms. "I'll ask someone. It's the Henry Ford principle. If you're not an expert in something, just find someone who is and ask them."

"And would Henry Ford have wasted time and resources ignoring the expert in front of him in order to find a *different* one, just because he didn't like her?"

"I'm sure he would have if the expert in front of him had told him to build a car out of gold instead of metal. And this has nothing to do with how I feel about you personally." There was a fraction of a moment's hesitation, then he added, "And I assume your antagonism toward me has nothing to do with your personal feelings, either."

"Of course not," she said, too quickly. "I have no personal feelings toward you."

"Good." His expression didn't change. Didn't even flicker. "Then we're just temporary business associates."

"Exactly." So why was she feeling stung by his pronouncement that he didn't feel anything toward her?

"Then we shouldn't have any more problems."

She splayed her arms. "No problems here. As long as you let me do my job the way I know it needs to be done."

"Fine. As long as you do it within the financial parameters I know you need."

She didn't answer.

For a moment they stood there, looking at each other like boxers between rounds.

Warren's gaze traveled to Rose's mouth, and she felt a tingle run right through her chest and stomach. For one crazy moment, she actually hoped he would kiss her.

And for one crazy moment, she actually thought he was going to.

He took a step forward and looked down into her upturned face. His eyes were bluer than she'd thought, and she was more vulnerable to his good looks than she wanted to be. The smell of his light but expensive cologne mingled in the air with decades of grease, making her want to move closer to him. But she resisted, thank goodness.

"Rose," he said in a low voice.

"Yes?" She could barely breathe.

"You're an excellent cook. And I appreciate that you want to do your best here, but this is just an old diner, not a five-star restaurant. Paying double for premium ingredients here is like putting diamonds in a rhinestone necklace. No one's going to notice the difference. Except me. And Doc, when he gets back and looks at the invoices."

Something inside of Rose deflated. Warren was a one-track guy, and that track was all business.

"You know," she said after a moment. "I'm sure in the business world, this bottom-line consciousness makes you successful, but out here in the real world, it really makes you difficult to deal with."

"I'm okay with that." He went back to the counter and returned his attention to the paperwork in front of him. *Dismissed,* his posture said.

You may go.

The king has spoken.

Rose watched him with disappointment, searching for some sort of comeback but nothing occurred to her. Instead she just said, "I'm going home now since I have to get up early and start cooking all that gold I ordered. You'll have to lock up here."

"Okay." He didn't look at her, he just kept studying the papers. He probably wasn't even aware that he'd offended her. Or he just didn't care. "You can go."

Dismissed.

She stood there looking at him for a moment. His wavy dark hair was mussed and she could see why. He kept punching numbers into his calculator, then sighing, shaking his head and dragging his hand through his hair. It was a habit of his that she'd already picked up on; he raked his hand through his hair when he was frustrated.

It was funny to see the great Warren Harker, millionaire—maybe even billionaire—sitting at the dingy Formica table trying to balance numbers that were probably smaller than his own entertainment budget. He could easily have written a check to bring everything into the black and never even missed the money. But he knew that Doc would never accept that kind of help. Which left him in the unusual and somewhat amusing, at least to Rose, position of having to make this tiny business succeed.

And since it ultimately benefited Doc, she felt no guilt whatsoever at taking satisfaction in seeing him struggle with it.

Chapter Six

Rose's cooking was excellent. Warren would grant her that. Doc's chili couldn't hold so much as a match to hers, much less a candle. Her burgers were juicy on the inside, with a tasty, crusty outside. Chicken salad? She raised it to a tender, rich delicacy. Strawberry shortcake? He'd never known it could be better than chocolate cake. The strawberries were the perfect combination of sweet and tart. The shortcake stuff was like a flaky, buttery biscuit. The cream on top was sweetened perfectly, like a European pastry, rather than the cloyingly sweet American version that was so sweet it tickled when you swallowed it.

Warren wasn't exactly a gourmand but Rose's cooking had him thinking of food as art.

Usually he wasn't that interested in either.

However, he wasn't ready to attribute the increase in business to her costly ingredients. She was still cutting the profit margin considerably. She could use ground chuck instead of ground sirloin and the food would taste pretty much the same. And the crowds of people? Given the unseasonably warm weather and consistently sunny days, Warren was pretty sure they'd be there anyway.

It was a coincidence that it was happening now.

Still, he was glad it was happening because what was good for the diner was good for Doc and Esther.

"*This* is the place you were telling me about?" Warren overhead a pregnant woman asking her companion, another young woman in the kind of stylish clothes one would associate more with Manhattan than this section of Brooklyn.

"I'm telling you, I've heard of two people going into labor after eating here. It's like magic."

"What did they eat?"

"Different things. I guess it's just some sort of spice they use here or something."

The pregnant woman patted her stomach. "Let's eat!"

Warren watched the two women scoot into a booth and eagerly pick up menus. He chuckled to himself. Whatever got the customers in, he figured, was good. But this was pretty silly. Rose's cooking didn't magically put women into labor.

Then he remembered something they'd talked about the night of his party, when he'd first met Rose. That artichoke salad Marta Serragno had chased him around with. It was supposed to be some sort of aphrodisiac or something.

He shook his head. If Rose was getting people to buy into this nonsense that her cooking was somehow magical, she was a much more clever marketing person than he'd given her credit for.

"Warren," Rose said, coming up to the booth. "I need to talk to you for a minute."

"Okay." He cleared some of the papers aside from his makeshift desk. "Have a seat."

She sat down and looked at him directly. "I need to hire some temporary help. Things are crazy here. It's too much."

Warren looked around. The place *was* full. And there were about six people waiting in the front for tables. But there weren't *that* many tables here. Surely Rose, Stu, Paul, Tim and Hap could work it out themselves. "There are five of you on staff. That's enough."

"It's *not* enough," she returned. "You can't expect these guys to work sixteen hour days, seven days a week."

"Look, the only thing that's different now than it was two weeks ago is that Doc's not here. So you're short one person. It's only temporary. Work it out."

She shook her head. "That isn't the only thing

that's different from two weeks ago and you know it. Have you ever seen the place this crowded?"

He hadn't. "It's just the nice weather."

She gave a skeptical scoff. "I don't care what it is, it's making for a heavy workload around here. We need help."

She was cute when she was mad. He knew better than to tell her that, but it was true. And he liked the fact that she didn't back down when he said no, even though his life would have been easier if she did.

"Okay, do you know anyone who might want a little bit of temporary work?"

Her smile was definitely satisfied. "When I worked for Serragno there was a part-timer named Deb who was always looking to pick up extra work. I think she lives near here."

He gave a concessionary shrug. "Fine. But make sure she knows it's temporary. I'll cover her salary myself, but you know as well as I do that Doc's not going to be able to afford that when he gets back."

"We'll see." She stood up and straightened her skirt. "At this rate, I'm not sure he'll be able to afford not to hire more help."

"It's the weather," Warren told her again.

"Okay." She started to walk away.

He indulged in the view of her backside for just a moment before stopping her. "Rose."

She turned back to him.

That was a good view, too.

"I need to get out of here now." His lawyer had told him it was time to get moving on the real estate across the street. If they were quick and made the right offer, they might be able to get it. "Think you can handle things from here?"

She nodded, a small smile playing at her lips. "As soon as you vacate one of my tables, my job gets easier."

When things finally slowed down later that night, Rose pulled out the phone book and looked up Deb Frey's number. The first two Freys she tried were wrong numbers, and the third hung up on her before she got a chance to ask if they knew of Deb.

As luck would have it, though, Deb happened to call Rose that night and Lily had given her the number for the diner. Deb said she'd heard Rose was working in the neighborhood and wondered if the restaurant needed any more help.

It was the greatest serendipity. Deb needed evening work on the weekdays, and that was the Cottage's busiest time. She agreed to start the next day.

Rose stretched her aching legs and yawned. This was hard work, but satisfying. Once she'd wanted to have her own catering business, but she was starting to think maybe it would be fun to have her own restaurant someday. She was really enjoying it.

Things had slowed down enough that she could let most of the guys go early. Half an hour before closing, the bells on the door rang and someone yelled. "Got room for a party of twelve?"

Rose sprang up and out of the kitchen to see the customers.

There was only one. Lily.

"Gotcha." Lily laughed. She set her purse down on the counter and said, "How about a cup of coffee for one?"

"You drink too much coffee," Rose said. "How about hot chocolate instead?"

"Mmm." Lily smiled. "Your recipe?"

"Actually, no. This just comes from a machine." Rose put a mug under the machine's nozzle and pushed the red button. Steaming hot chocolate poured into the cup, foaming on top. She handed it to Lily. "It's actually pretty good, though."

Lily took a sip. "You're right, it is." She set the cup down. "So how's it going? I've barely seen you for more than a week."

"I know." Rose sat on the stool next to her. The soles of her feet tingled when she took her weight off them. "It's been nonstop here."

"I'm not surprised. You're the best cook on the east coast."

"Hardly."

Lily raised an eyebrow. "I'm not kidding. You don't know how great you are."

"Oh, come on. Give me a break."

Lily shook her head, her golden hair gleaming

even under the horrible fluorescent lights. "Sometimes I wonder if you're lacking self-esteem because we didn't have our parents when we grew up."

"I'm not lacking self-esteem!"

"You never take enough credit for what you do, you let jerks like Marta Serragno take advantage of you and take credit for your work, and you never demand to be paid what you're worth."

Rose laughed. "Okay, I know I'm worth more than I'm getting paid here, but if you recall it wasn't like I could get a job elsewhere."

Lily shrugged. "I bet Warren Harker would have hired you."

"To do what?"

"Private chef?"

Rose rolled her eyes. "For one thing, I doubt he even *has* a chef, and for another, he and I aren't exactly the best of pals."

"There's another thing." Lily pointed at her. "You aren't confident enough with men."

Easy for Lily to say. Men swarmed around her, like bees to honey. Anyone would look as if they were lacking confidence next to that. But she knew this wasn't really just about her. Lily often brought up the fact that they had grown up without parents, so whatever loss they felt, they both felt it. "You think about them a lot, don't you?" Rose said.

"Our parents?"

Rose nodded. "Yes. Don't you?"

"I try not to focus on the loss, but, sure, of course I think about them. It feels like something's missing."

"I feel exactly the same way. Like there's a part of me that will never be whole because of the loss."

"Well, it's pretty obvious what," Lily said. "I mean, we've been without our parents since we were under two years old. It's not a mystery that we should feel like something's missing."

"I know, I know," Rose said. But she still felt the faint feeling of loss. "Is it normal to feel like whatever's missing is just out of my reach? Do you feel that way, too?"

"Yes," Lily said, pulling Rose in for a tight hug. "Of course I do. But, come on, it's normal."

"I guess."

There were times that called for chocolate and this was one of them. Rose got herself a mug and filled it with hot chocolate. "That's natural, I'm sure," she said. "It doesn't mean we're *not* whole. We just miss them. But, hey, at least we have each other!"

"You bet." Lily reached over and gave her a hug. "Ready to go home?"

Rose looked around the place. Everything was done, it was all set up for the morning. That gave her—she looked at her watch—just about seven hours to sleep. If she started right now. "More than ready," she said. "Let's go."

Chapter Seven

It was just bad luck for Rose the next night when, just as Warren was finishing his exacting scrutiny of the day's profits and losses, one of the pipes under the sink burst.

She was cleaning up the last pot and counting the moments until she got home and into her bed, when she heard a small, spitting hiss under the sink. She turned off the water and looked under the sink.

At first, she didn't see anything and was about to chalk it up to the normal sounds of the drain when the spitting sound got louder.

Then she saw it.

A trickle of glistening water was raining down on the pans beneath the sink.

She reached for the knob in the back and tried to turn the water off. It wouldn't budge. She gathered her strength and gave it a hard yank, but nothing happened.

Rose muttered an oath and hurried to the supply cabinet to find some kind of wrench or crowbar or something that she could use to try and turn the rusted handle, but the only thing she found was a broken handle from a large saucepan.

She took the handle back to the sink and worked it in between the spokes of the handle. It still wouldn't budge. Even when she put all of her weight into it and tried to lever it, all that happened was the stainless steel pan handle began to bend.

This was really bad timing.

She went back to the supply cabinet, hoping to find some duct tape to seal the leak while she called a plumber. Unfortunately, the supply cabinet contained little more than spare aprons, towels, and miscellaneous barware. There was nothing resembling a tool or tape.

She took an apron and went back to the sink. Carefully she reached in and tried to tie the apron around the pipe; but the copper was old and corroded and the minute she touched it, it crumbled beneath her fingers.

Suddenly the trickle became a real leak.

Muttering a word that would have shocked Sister Gladys at the Barrie Home, Rose hurriedly pulled the pans out from under the sink.

"What's all the racket?" Warren asked.

Under the sink, Rose paused for just a second and closed her eyes. She didn't want him to know about this. He'd already been so condescending about her supposedly extravagant food purchases and then her needing to hire extra help that if he suspected she was at fault for having to call the plumber, she'd never hear the end of it.

She took a short, bracing breath, then came out from under the sink. "I'm just...rearranging things."

"Now?"

"Why not?"

"You were just talking about how exhausted you were. You threatened to sleep in and make me open up and make eggs in the morning."

She smiled. "I was only kidding."

He lowered his brow. "You were kidding."

"Yes. Just, you know, making light of things because you were so nasty about me hiring extra help."

"I wasn't nasty about it, Rose, I was just trying to save Doc some money."

Next to her, the water pooled in a pan and began to make a subtle splashing sound.

"You know, you're right," she said, giving what she hoped was a sincere-looking smile. "I think it's really nice the way you think about that. Not that I was wrong, mind you." She wasn't going to give him that, no matter what was going on with the sink next to her. "But I'm really glad you're here to take care of that kind of thing so I can just worry about the cooking."

The look that came over his face was definitely suspicious. "So you're saying you *appreciate* me."

"Uh-huh." The dripping got louder. She figured she had two, maybe three minutes before the pan began to overflow.

"You appreciate what I'm doing here."

She nodded. "Absolutely. So, to that end, you should probably go on home and get some sleep. After all you're working two jobs. Gotta have enough sleep."

He didn't move. "You're trying to get rid of me."

"No, I'm not."

"Yes, you are."

She clicked her tongue against her teeth. "Warren, why would I be trying to get rid of you?"

"That's what I'd like to know." He looked her over, then looked at the sink.

"That's crazy."

He returned his gaze to her. "Why don't you get up for a minute?"

She cleared her throat. "Up?"

"Yeah, up."

"But I'm in the middle of something here." She looked at the pipe; the leak was getting worse. "I may not be tired," she lied, "but I can't stay here all night. I just want to finish what I'm doing and go home." And *that* was the truth.

Warren walked slowly toward her, stopping directly in front of her. His expensive Italian leather shoes looked out of place on the scuffed linoleum floor. If he didn't get them out of here quick, they were going to be ruined. "What, exactly, are you doing?" He bent down and looked.

She closed her eyes and said a half-hearted prayer that he wouldn't notice the pipe.

It didn't work.

She saw him reaching for the pipe, and barely got out the words, "Don't touch the pipe," before he did just that.

"What the hell—" He reached out and grasped it, and the entire pipe gave way in his hand. Water sprayed everywhere, soaking Rose's shirt and Warren's hair and costly suit.

"You shouldn't have done that!" Rose said, scrambling to her feet.

He looked at her, water spraying against him. "You think?"

"Quick! We have to get some stock pots to catch the water!"

Instead of following suit, he knelt in front of the sink. "There should be a cutoff valve under here."

"I tried that. It didn't work."

"What do you mean, it didn't work? It cuts off the water."

She gestured at the geyser. "It didn't work. I couldn't get it to move."

A look she recognized as He-Man to the Rescue came over his face, and he reached into the back to turn the valve.

"It won't move," he said after a few minutes.

"I told you that."

"We need a tool."

"There aren't any."

Irritation crossed his face, then his eyes lit on the broken pan handle she'd left several feet away. "Let me have that thing."

"I tried that, too."

He didn't even try to hide his exasperation. "How long have you been *playing* around with this?"

She put her hands on her hips. "I would hardly say I've been playing with it. After all, I did everything you've tried, and I did it first. Except breaking the pipe all the way through, that is."

"So this is my fault?"

"No, but it's not mine, either."

"Rose," he said calmly, the water spewing toward him in an arc, like a summer sprinkler.

"Yes?"

"Can we argue the details of this later and stop this damn water before we have to build an ark?"

She couldn't help but laugh. "I'll get some pots." She hurried to get the largest stock pots in the place and positioned them to catch most of the water.

Meanwhile, Warren peeled off his expensive suit jacket.

"Take the shoes off, too," Rose suggested. "They're going to be ruined."

"I don't care about that," he said, looking at her like she was crazy.

"Okay," she said. "Just don't say I didn't warn you."

He gave a nod. "Duly noted. So what do you say you call a plumber?"

"Oh! Jeez, of course. Hang on, just—" she gestured toward the mess "—keep an eye on things."

He gave a wry smile. "No problem."

She went to the phone and dialed information to find the nearest plumber. She was given three numbers, and the first two were out on calls and weren't expected to be back anytime soon. Fortunately, the third, Grim Brothers Plumbing and Heating, were available, and she was told the plumber would be there within half an hour.

She hung up the phone and returned to Warren, who was emptying one stock pot into the sink, while the other seemed to be filling at twice the speed it had been when Rose had left.

"It's getting worse," she said.

He nodded. "How long before someone gets here?"

"Could be as long as half an hour."

He sighed. "Okay. I have an idea. Keep an eye on this and I'll be right back." He went into the bathroom in the back and returned a few minutes later with a length of pipe. "Don't worry," he said, in answer to her unasked question. "It's not flooding in there now."

She had to laugh. "So what's the plan?"

"Behold," he said with a pirate smile.

She raised her eyebrows and stepped aside while he fought his way through the stream of water to the pipes beneath the sink.

"Can I get you anything?"

"A large scotch and a small soda."

"How about something to help fix the pipe?"

"Yeah, bring me that, too." He shifted his position, knocked his head and cussed. "And you might want to prepare an ice pack for when this is all over."

"I've got a big bag of frozen lima beans with your name on it," she said.

"Ugh." He laughed, and worked some more. Soon the stream of water grew smaller, and, finally, disappeared altogether.

He pulled out of the cabinet with complaints about his aching back and then stood up, wiping his hands on the front of his pants. "There."

She was amazed. "You fixed it!"

"I'm not completely useless at manual labor." He began to roll his sleeves up and only then did she notice how his wet shirt clung to what turned out to be a Greek-god-like masculine form.

She smiled. "I am seriously impressed. With your plumbing, I mean," she hastened to add, lest he should think she was ogling him.

Which she was.

He smiled back. "Thank you. It's all in a day's work."

Just then, the hiss began again. Rose recognized it immediately.

"Look out!" she cried. "The pipe blew!"

He raised a questioning glance one second before the water hit him in the face. When he took a step to get away, he slipped and crashed to the floor.

Rose gasped. "Are you okay?" She hurried over to help him up but when she got close, she slipped on the same slick spot he had and went toppling down on top of him.

"Are *you* okay?" he asked, grabbing her in his arms.

"Yes, I just came to help you up."

"Good job."

They looked at each other and burst out laughing.

"The kitchen's getting soaked," Rose said at last, starting to get up.

He held her in place. "Let it," he said. "I'll buy a new one."

"A new kitchen?"

"Or a new ark. Whichever we need more when this is over."

They laughed again.

But Rose's mirth turned to something else when she looked at him, all wet and rumpled and gorgeous. She had the irrational urge to kiss him.

And when he looked at her and his smile faded just a fraction, she thought he might want the same thing.

"You know, you even look beautiful when you're wet," he commented, running his hands up her arms.

She felt her face grow warm. "You're not going to get out of being teased for this just by flattering me." She pulled back and struggled to her feet.

"I wouldn't dare," he answered, a dimple denting his cheek. But his eyes didn't reflect the same open amusement that they had just a few minutes earlier.

Rose's breath was caught in her throat. She didn't know what to do. If she gave in and kissed him, it would be nice in the short run, but in the long run it could only lead to hurt.

If, on the other hand, she just walked away, who knew how long she would feel this dull ache in her chest?

She left it up to Warren.

Without speaking, he lowered his mouth onto hers.

His lips touched hers lightly at first, teasing, tantalizing. Rose leaned into the kiss, then paused. For a moment, neither moved. Their breath mingled between them, an entity unto itself, begging their attention.

Rose looked into Warren's eyes and it was all over. His mouth sought hers out again, this time more intense, hungrier. When his tongue made contact with hers, an electrical frisson of desire racked her body.

She trailed her hands up his arms and pulled him closer to her, eagerly exploring his mouth with her own, tasting his taste and smelling his scent.

Warren pressed his hands down her back, stopping at the small of her back. His hands played at the elastic band of her panties, and even though she knew things couldn't possibly go further, Rose leaned into him, reveling in the pleasurable sensations. He carefully lowered her back against the counter, the cold Formica hitting her skin with what felt like a sizzle.

She was ready. She wanted him. There was no turning back now.

"Did someone here call a plumber?"

The voice started both Rose and Warren out of their embrace.

"Yes," Warren said, removing his hands from Rose quickly, as if they'd never been there. "There's a—a—" He pointed at the sink, and the water flowing from it. "Some sort of leak. As you can see."

The plumber, who was clearly trying not to smile, gave a nod. "Mind if I start to work on it?"

"Go right ahead," Rose said quickly. Blood rushed into her cheeks and burned like charcoal. "Please."

"You can go," Warren said to her quietly, giving a nod. "My driver is out front. Tell him your address and he'll take you home."

She ran her hand through her hair, trying to straighten her appearance. "But you shouldn't have to wait here."

"I have to anyway," he said firmly. "I have to write the check."

There was no way for her to argue with that. It wasn't as if she could stay and take care of it. "Are you sure you don't mind?" Part of her hoped he would say he wanted her to stay. To pick up things right where they'd left off as soon as the plumber had gone.

But the mood was broken, and they both knew it.

"Go. Get some sleep."

"Okay, then," she said uncertainly. "I'll see you…later, I guess."

He gave a quick, professional smile. Their moment was clearly over. "I'll be around."

"Okay," she said again. "Thanks for the ride."

He nodded in a way that suggested *anytime* and she went on her way, feeling slightly bemused.

The ride home was short, but it was long enough for her to realize that she didn't want to have this kind of uncertainty in her life. Yes, Warren had kissed her but she didn't know what it meant, or even if it meant anything at all. The man was a notorious playboy and she would have to be a fool to think he was interested in something long-term.

She could always ask him, of course, but if she did she would only be exposing her own vulnerability. She would be putting herself out there to a man who was in a different league and knew it. It wasn't that he was *better* than she was, she didn't believe that for a moment, but he was wealthy. And the rich, she had learned time and again, *were* different. She and Warren may have some pretty steamy chemistry going on now and then, but they didn't have anything in common. She was a working-class girl from Brooklyn. He was a high-stakes player and winner in Manhattan. There was no middle ground for them.

It was better to just leave it as it was now. A pleasant but brief encounter between two people who had lost their heads under extenuating circumstances.

Nothing else would happen.

Rose would make sure of it.

Chapter Eight

In the days that followed, Warren and Rose had a much easier rapport with each other. He teased her about overpaying for organic toothpicks, and she teased him for pinching his pennies so hard she could hear Lincoln screaming.

They also worked together when they needed to, balancing the books and reconciling the daily slips, as well as donating leftover food at the end of each day to a local soup kitchen. As soon as Rose had pointed out it would be a tax write-off, Warren was all for it, and it had helped counterbalance what she was spending on higher quality ingredients.

All in all, after a couple of quiet weeks, Rose began to feel as if she and Warren were actually friends. They ended up on opposite sides of a lot of fences, but even when they argued, they usually ended up laughing in the end.

But they didn't talk about the kiss again. Rose tried not to take it personally, and rationalized to herself that he had probably reached the same conclusion she had about the two of them. Their lives were too different, and getting together romantically could only complicate the business relationship they were forced to have right now.

When a package arrived for Warren one afternoon in mid-October, it surprised Rose. Granted, he'd placed several orders in his own name so that Doc wouldn't be charged for them. But this one was different. The box was small, about eight inches high and wide, and a foot long. It had arrived via courier, but there was no return address.

As soon as she had a moment, she went into the back, took out the business card Warren had given her and made a call to his office. The secretary who answered said he was in a meeting and took a message, so Rose set the box aside and went back to work.

Warren returned her call around 7 p.m.

"A box came for you," she said, trying to sound nonchalant. He'd probably thought she was calling for personal reasons, so she was quick to let him know she wasn't.

"Did you open it?"

"Of course not. It has your name on it."

He sighed. "If it came to the diner, then it's something for the diner. Open it up."

"Fine, fine. Hold on." She set the receiver down and retrieved the box. It was tightly sealed with packing tape, so she had to get a knife. When she'd finally wrestled the thing open, she found another box inside. This one was marked Confidential. She returned to the phone and told Warren.

"Confidential?" he repeated.

"That's what it says. In big black letters."

"Was there any sort of return address? Anything at all that might indicate where it came from?"

She looked again. "Nope. Just a plain brown box. You haven't purchased something that requires…discretion, have you?"

"No." He was clearly not up for joking. "How big is the box?"

"Small. Like eight inches long, five inches wide, and maybe five inches tall. It's obviously not, you know, produce or anything." She gave a small laugh.

There was a pause, then he said, "Look, I hate to ask you this, but if I send a car do you think you can bring it up here?"

"To Manhattan?"

"Is that a problem?"

"The place is packed. It's dinner time."

"Your friend is working there, right? So you can cut out a couple of hours early. Let Hap lock up."

"I don't know." She looked around doubtfully.

She hated to leave everyone with extra work when the place was still so busy. "Can't it wait until tomorrow?"

"Maybe not," Warren said. His voice was tight with tension. "Please."

His tone got her attention. "Okay. Give me an hour."

"I'll see you then." He hung up.

The hour passed quickly, and she was still waiting for her apple pies to come out of the oven when Warren's driver showed up. She told Hap to take the pies out in another five minutes, reminded him again that he was in charge of locking the diner at the end of the night, then took the box and got into the sleek black limo that Warren had sent.

The seats were buttery smooth leather, and there was a bottle of champagne in an ice bucket with a single flute next to it. The radio was softly playing an old Beatles tune.

She could get used to this.

Well, no, she couldn't. Obviously this wasn't going to become her life, but still there was something so relaxing about sitting in this quiet, smooth car on buttery soft leather seats. It was like a sensory deprivation chamber. The noise of the city receded into the background outside the tinted glass windows.

After a ride that didn't last nearly long enough, the car pulled up outside the Wyoming apartment building, and the driver got out and opened the door for her. He gave a slight bow as she thanked him for the ride. She had barely taken three steps before a doorman in a tall hat and tails gave a similar bow and opened the door to the building for her.

The lobby was as quiet as a tomb, and it was a stark contrast to the noise she had just left outside. But buildings like this prided themselves on offering silence to the wealthy weary.

She approached the security desk. "Hello, I'm here to see Warren Harker."

"You are Miss Tilden?"

"Yes."

"Miss Tilden, Mr. Harker is expecting you."

The guard told her to take the private elevator to the penthouse, and he gave her a code to punch into the keypad in order to do so.

She pushed the button and the elevator doors opened almost immediately to reveal a gilded box, with mirrored walls and only three floors to choose from. She pushed Penthouse, entered the code number the doorman had given her, and the doors shushed closed, allowing the box to shoot upwards at breathtaking speed.

Before she knew it, the doors opened and she found herself stepping into the marble foyer of what looked like the set from a 1940s high-budget musical.

"What took you so long?"

"Sorry, the traffic wouldn't part for me like the Red Sea, the way it undoubtedly does for you. It took me a while to get uptown."

"Funny. Listen, I got a call. Good news—Doc's gone home to recuperate now. He's out of the woods."

Rose hadn't realized that Doc was actually *in* the woods after she'd seen him, so she was extremely glad to hear that there was no real danger to him now.

"When will he go back to work?"

"Unfortunately, that's still some weeks away. Is that the package you were telling me about?" He nodded toward the box she had forgotten she was holding.

"Yes." She handed it to him, then looked around in awe at floor-to-ceiling windows that overlooked Central Park on one side, and Radio City Music Hall on the other. "Is this where you actually live?"

He examined the box. "As opposed to…?"

"Well, the hotel suite you were using when Marta Serragno catered for you."

"Nah, this is where I live," he said distractedly, working the tape off the box. "The suite is just a convenient place to host events. It seems personal without actually giving anything of myself away."

She looked at him, surprised at his acute self-awareness. "So I've been allowed into the inner sanctum, so to speak?"

He looked up at her, smiled mischievously for a moment, then said, simply, "Not yet."

The way he said it sent shivers running down her spine.

"Yet?"

"You never know what's going to happen."

She raised an eyebrow. "We're just business associates. And even that is temporary."

"True. I don't have any intention of staying in the restaurant business. It's too much work for too little profit."

She shrugged. "Like most things, you really have to have your heart in it, or there's no point."

"Is your heart in it?"

"What, in the Cottage?"

"Yeah. Your work there."

"Yes," she said. "Yes, it is."

"Then Doc's damn lucky to have you."

"So are you," she said, intending it as a joke then realizing how it sounded. "In the sense that you're helping Doc out, that is."

He looked at her for a long moment, in a way that made her skin prickle, then nodded. "It hasn't exactly been a hardship hanging out with you, anyway."

She smiled. "You didn't seem to feel that way when you looked over the invoices."

"Things changed after that."

She met his eyes. "Did they?"

He returned her gaze evenly. "Didn't they?"

She felt warmth rise in her cheeks. "Things aren't really going to change between us," she forced herself to say. "Regardless of what happens, I'm never going to be a socialite." She smiled. "And you're never going to be a plumber."

"Hey. I did all right. For a few minutes, anyway. Besides, what makes you think I'd want you to be a socialite?"

She thought about how to answer. "Your résumé. Your life."

"What do you know about my life?"

"It's a matter of public record, isn't it? I bet a day doesn't pass that you're not mentioned somewhere in the New York papers."

"Maybe." He cocked his head slightly and said, "But you don't know the whole story."

That sounded interesting. "Do you want to tell me the whole story then?"

Three heartbeats passed.

"I don't know," he said at last.

What could she say to that? "Open your package," she said, walking to the window so he couldn't see the flush she knew was rising her cheeks. "You made me come all the way over here with it, the least you could do is tell me what it is." She stopped and looked down at 48th Street below.

Cars were inching forward in small increments, horns blaring, headlights flashing. Even though it was late, the sidewalks were pulsing with pedestrians. It was the heartbeat of the city, the sound of life playing itself out on the stage of life fifty floors down.

Rose could have watched it for hours except that she was interrupted by a very unholy oath from Warren across the room.

"What's wrong?" Rose asked, turning to him.

He was looking down into the plain brown box which he had gotten open.

He cursed again.

"What *is* it?"

"This," he said, tipping the box toward her.

She looked but she couldn't tell what the lump inside of it was. But before she could ask, he supplied her with the answer.

"It's a dead rat," he said, setting the box down on the table by the sofa.

"A dead *rat?*" she repeated, thinking she must have heard him incorrectly.

But he nodded grimly.

"Why? Who would send that?" She was sputtering with surprise and disgust.

"Someone's sending me a message, and I don't like it. I don't like it one bit."

Chapter Nine

"What message?" Rose asked, hurrying toward him. "Let me see that."

He blocked her before she could get to the box and look inside for herself. "You don't want to see it."

She glanced over his shoulder at the box and decided he was right, she didn't need to see a dead animal. "Well, what does it mean? Why would someone send that to you?"

"The same reason they'd rough up Doc," he said, anguish etched in his features. "It's a warning."

A chill ran through Rose. It hadn't immediately occurred to her that this might be connected with what had happened to Doc. "What's the warning?"

she asked. "Be kind to animals? Drive older men home? It makes no sense."

Warren looked into her eyes, the blue of his own dark and troubled. "Unfortunately, it makes complete sense. Someone's telling me to keep my business out of the neighborhood or else innocent people could get hurt."

"What's your business?" Rose wanted to know. "Are you doing something illegal?" It was the only explanation she could think of for these heavy-handed, thug-style threats.

"Of course not."

"Well, these aren't altar boys asking you to keep out of their flower gardens." She gestured toward the box. "This stuff is ugly. What kind of people are these?"

Warren was silent for a long time before finally giving a single nod and saying, "They're not altar boys. You're right. But they're also not regular businessmen, because things never would have escalated this way if they were."

"Not regular businessmen?"

He shook his head.

"So what are you?" she asked, almost afraid to hear his answer.

A half smile tugged at the corner of his mouth. "I'm a legitimate businessman."

"With some pretty ugly adversaries."

He glanced behind him at the box containing the rat, then nodded at Rose. "Admittedly."

"Well, Warren—" this was such a no-brainer, she

almost couldn't believe she had to ask "—you're going to do what they want, right?"

He looked surprised. "No way."

No? "You're going to let this continue just so you can make some money?"

"It's not just about money."

"I don't care what it's about, Doc could have been killed!" She thought of the other hapless fellows who worked and patronized the diner. They weren't exactly superheroes in disguise. So many of them would be physically vulnerable if thugs tried to hurt them. "You're putting a lot of innocent people in danger!"

He shook his head and looked at her intensely. "These people are in the neighborhood. They're dangerous. The reason they're concerned about me developing there is because they want to continue doing whatever illegal activity it is that they're doing."

She wanted to believe him, but she couldn't bear the thought of Stu or Hap or any of the others getting injured. She walked back to the window and looked down at the relative safety that was midtown Manhattan. "At least no one was getting hurt or threatened before."

Warren came up behind her. "When people like that are controlling a neighborhood, *no one* is safe. Believe me." He was so close that the heat from his body penetrated her clothes. "As for the diner, I'll hire private security to hang around. You'll be safe, don't worry."

She turned to him, surprised that he was a couple of feet away. She'd felt as if he were closer. "I'm not worried about myself. I'm worried about the others."

He looked at her in silence for a moment, then smiled. "You're something, you know that?"

The timbre of his voice gave her pause. Suddenly she wasn't sure what to say. "Is that a good thing or a bad thing?"

He took a step toward her, closing the gap between them by half. "It's a good thing." He touched his finger to her jaw, lifting her chin so she was looking directly into his face. "It's a really good thing."

She didn't draw back. She didn't want to. "That's about the last thing I expected to hear *you* say."

He chuckled softly. "I gotta tell you, I wasn't expecting to say it myself."

Her breath caught in her chest. "Watch out. We don't want anyone getting the wrong impression."

"No one can see us."

She swallowed. "Then we don't want *us* getting the wrong impression either, do we?"

He didn't move. Didn't back off. "What's the wrong impression?"

"That we're…" She cleared her throat. "You know…*involved*. Romantically." She looked at his mouth, felt her chest flutter, then turned her attention to his eyes. "Interested in each other."

"Ah. I see. So…" He ran his thumb along her cheek. "What's the right impression?"

She did not have an answer for that. It was hard to call them friends. *Business associates* would have been a mischaracterization. "Acquaintances?" she offered, closing her eyes for a moment against the tingle his touch sent through her.

There was a smile in his voice as he said, "That's a start."

He didn't move his hand from her face.

And she didn't want him to.

She parted her lips and realized she'd been holding her breath. "A start?"

"Well, technically I guess you could say we already had a start, a few weeks ago."

She swallowed. "You could also say that was an aberration."

He took a step toward her. "An aberration?"

"A moment of weakness?"

"Hmm."

"Stockholm syndrome?"

He laughed and reached out to put his hands on her shoulders. "Or maybe just basic attraction," he said, looking down into her eyes.

She took a wavering breath. "Maybe."

"Is there anything wrong with that?"

"Maybe."

He raised an eyebrow, then lowered his mouth onto hers and drew her into a searing kiss.

It was unlike any kiss she'd ever had. Where other men were hungry or fumbling or eager to move onto "bigger and better things," Warren had kissing down to an art. He moved his hand softly across her jaw and through her hair, sending a path of tingles along behind it.

With his other hand, he pulled her close against his hard, muscular body. She melted against the masculine landscape, wrapping her arms around him and pressing her palms against his back. She could feel his muscles move under her touch. It was a delicious sensation.

Her body immediately flamed to life in response. Never in her life had she wanted so much, so fast. It was as if she were drowning and Warren's kiss was the air she needed to breathe. She didn't want it to end. Ever.

He parted her lips with his, deepening the kiss. It was a tantalizingly slow process that sent a bud of desire blooming from the pit of her stomach into her breast and pelvis. It would be easy to go too far with a man like this.

Too easy.

Somewhere in the back of her mind, a small voice nagged at her conscience. She couldn't let this happen. She couldn't become just another notch in his belt.

She drew back, breathless. "I don't think that's what acquaintances do."

"Then we need a new label." He pulled her back against him and kissed her mouth, her jaw, her neck...

She leaned her head back, enjoying the sensation and the alluring scent of him for a moment, before, once again, she pulled away. "I don't think this is helping us help Doc."

He shrugged. "It's not hurting, either."

"I have a feeling it could if we don't stop."

"Yeah?" He ran her hair through his fingertips, looking at it admiringly before turning that bedroom-blue gaze back to her eyes. "You'd consider not stopping?"

Her face went warm. "I didn't mean that."

He cocked his head fractionally. "But you said it. You don't strike me as a woman who says anything she doesn't mean."

She took a step back and felt the cool window against her back. "And you don't strike me as a man who doesn't get what he wants. I guess we're both going to have to go against character for now. For Doc's sake," she hastened to add.

Warren put his hands up in mock surrender. "You win. I'll even acknowledge that you're probably right. We don't need to complicate things any more than they already are. This—" he gestured toward the box "—message, or whatever you want to call it, really ticks me off. I'm going to have to move a lot faster on my plans than I had intended."

She couldn't believe what he was saying. "Are you serious?"

"Completely."

"But won't that just make your—your enemies even angrier? What if they hurt someone else?"

"I told you I'd increase security in the neighborhood."

"I'm not sure that's good enough."

"It's all I can do."

"You can stop with your plans."

"No, I can't." His voice was low and smooth. And so quietly confident that she was tempted to just believe him and let him take care of everything in his own way. "And as I already explained to you, that wouldn't help matters anyway. You're safer with me there than without me."

Again, his words sent shivers down her spine. "I'm not sure that's true."

He looked at her, his expression heavy with unspoken meaning. "You're going to have to trust me."

She gave a dry laugh. "It's not the first time I've heard that."

"It's the first time you've heard it from me," he said. "And I'm a man of my word." He caught her arm and pulled her closer, looking down into her eyes. "Trust me."

She swallowed hard. "I'll try."

He looked at her steadily for a moment, before cocking his head slightly and releasing his hold on her. "Okay, then."

"I'd better go," she said, in a voice that trembled slightly.

He splayed his arms. "I'll call the driver."

"I can take a cab."

"I brought you here, so I'm taking care of getting you back home. You're not taking some grungy cab."

She sighed. "Okay. Thanks."

He went to the phone and gave instructions for the car to be brought around to the front of the building.

Rose listened, impressed by how smooth he was, how completely in control of every situation. That was probably the thing that had caused her to lose her head with him, not once but twice. All her life, Rose had felt as if she had to take care of everything herself. Especially in relationships. Most men she dated tended to dote on her so much that they left every decision up to her, believing they were being accommodating rather than piling the responsibility on her.

It was nice to be around a man who took command now and then.

When Warren hung up the phone, he turned to Rose and said, "I'll walk you downstairs."

"Oh, no, you don't have to do that."

"I know I don't." He went to the door and opened it.

Rose went through and he accompanied her to the elevator.

The box seemed a lot smaller than it had when she'd ridden up on it. "Close quarters," she commented.

He glanced around, then gave a small smile but said nothing.

The heat from his body came at her in waves, like tendrils of energy snaking under her clothing and touching her body.

He smelled great, too.

She watched the digital numbers descend slowly as they passed the building floors. Forty-one, forty, thirty-nine. It seemed to be taking forever. Rose felt as if she couldn't breath. Her skin rose in prickly goose bumps and she half wished he'd just push the Penthouse button and take her back up. But as it was, she wasn't about to suggest it, so instead she stood beside him in the enclosed space and waited breathlessly for the moment she could say a quick goodbye and go outside into the cool air alone.

It wasn't a cold shower, but it would have to do.

Warren stood on the street and watched the car drive Rose back to Brooklyn. He stood, lost in thought, long after it had turned the corner and disappeared from sight.

It had been years since he'd known anyone even remotely like Rose. Once he'd moved uptown, he'd lost touch with the kind of people he'd grown up with downtown. The crime of it was that it had been all his own fault—he'd been so determined to succeed in his business, that he'd let everything else fall by the wayside. That kind of tunnel vision could win a man a lot of money, but it hadn't won him any friends.

Funny thing was, until he'd met Rose he hadn't realized how much he missed real people who would tell him what they thought, whether he wanted to hear it or not. Rose wasn't bowled over by his money because she didn't need it. Not from him.

She didn't need anything from him.

Which was the very thing that made him feel as if he needed to keep her around.

But he couldn't. He knew that. If he were to hire her in any capacity, she'd lose the very detachment that he valued so much. And if he were to get involved with her on a personal level…well, that just wasn't going to happen. Probably. Because he didn't have the time to devote to any sort of romantic relationship, and there was no way he could carve the time out of his schedule. Probably.

Especially given the time he had lost by having to go to the diner and take care of Doc's business.

"Excuse me, Mr. Harker?" The doorman's voice startled him out of his thoughts.

He turned.

"Is everything all right, Mr. Harker?"

"Fine. Thanks. Everything's fine." He gave a brief nod and started past the man.

When he opened the door to his apartment five minutes later, the phone was ringing. He wasn't in the mood to talk to anyone, so he let the call go to voice mail, but when it rang again immediately, he decided it could be important.

And it was. Mark Benning was on the phone.

"Score," Benning said without preamble.

Warren smiled. "You got the property."

"Have I ever failed you? I've got the contracts for you to sign right now."

"Call the courier," Warren said, his chest thrumming with the familiar thrill of winning. "This can't wait."

"You know it. The word got out quick that the place might be available. Offers are pouring in and from what I can tell, Apex is leading the pack."

Warren's stomach tightened. Larry Perkins, the president of Apex, was known to go into brutal territory when it came to getting what he wanted. No one was safe.

And he'd lost out to Warren one too many times, which made this personal as well as financial.

It was a bad combination.

"I don't trust Perkins," Warren said.

"Me, neither," Benning said. "I'm not going to feel good until this deal is signed, sealed and delivered. In fact, I'll just bring the papers over tonight myself and they'll be ratified first thing tomorrow."

"I'll be here."

"Good. I'll see you in twenty minutes. Get the scotch out, because this deal just about snapped my nerves."

"You got it. Excellent work, Benning." Warren replaced the receiver. He'd done it. He'd gotten the property. He'd gotten the building permits. This was going to be one of his most profitable ventures yet; as soon as the contracts were ratified, he could begin work breaking ground.

He wouldn't announce his plans until later, of course. When construction was almost complete, then he'd do a formal unveiling.

And it would be too late for the competition to compete.

Chapter Ten

"Word is spreading that you've got the magic touch," Deb said to Rose at the diner the next day.

Rose's former coworker from Serragno had been working there since the day after Doc's injury, and had seen the crowd go from nothing to packed in that short a time.

"Well, my supposed magic touch is getting a little burned out." Rose smiled. "Thank goodness you're here."

Deb smiled. "When you called it was, like, I don't know, kismet or something. Your timing was absolutely perfect."

"Serragno hasn't got much work for you?"

Deb shrugged. "Let's just say this is the perfect

complement to my work for Serragno. Two pay-checks *and* I get to learn the secrets of Rose Tilden's magical cooking. Sounds like a deal to me."

Rose laughed, though talk of her cooking as "magic" always made her uncomfortable. "Given the amount of work you've had to take on here, I'm very glad to hear you say that."

And indeed, the place was busy. It seemed as if every single day there was a marked increase in the number of customers. Word got out that Rose's salad could send pregnant women into labor, her soups could make men propose and her apple pie had made at least two people win the lottery, although not the Mega Millions jackpot.

Rose was feeling pretty good about the turn of events and what it could mean for Doc's business until a few mornings after her conversation with Deb, when she was getting ready to open the place.

A movement across the street caught her eye. All that was there was an enormous abandoned building and she rarely saw anyone near it. Until recently, the only sign of life there was a dry cleaner who never seemed to do any business, so the fact that anyone was there was a surprise. The fact that they were there at six in the morning made it even more so.

Rose went to the window and looked out. The morning light was just beginning to peek over the buildings, so the entire landscape was cast in shades of gray, but it was unmistakable that two people were standing on the corner, looking in the direction of the diner. There was a large man, built like a linebacker with wide shoulders and a protruding gut, and a tall, narrow woman whose hair was covered by a scarf.

But when the woman turned to face the diner, Rose's stomach dropped.

The woman was Marta Serragno.

At first, Rose thought it was her imagination, but she watched the couple for a moment and realized, without a doubt, that the spidery, sharp-featured woman couldn't be anyone else.

Marta and the heavyset blond man took several surreptitious glances at the Cottage Diner while they spoke. This would have been alarming under any circumstances, but something told Rose these weren't ordinary circumstances.

There seemed only one explanation. Marta was there because of Rose.

This was a woman whose jealousy knew no bounds. Marta didn't like to be upstaged, and if word of Rose's cooking had traveled beyond a few local blocks—and the increased business indicated it had—Marta was likely to hear. If she was still holding her grudge against Rose, it would be just like her to come to Brooklyn to try to sabotage her work here.

And if she heard that Rose was working closely with Warren Harker, it was a certainty that Marta was still holding her grudge.

All of these thoughts chased each other through

Rose's mind, while an eerie dread settled in the pit of her stomach.

"What's going on?"

Deb's voice behind Rose startled her, and when she turned to face her, it must have shown.

"Wow, you're as white as a ghost," Deb said. "What the heck is going on?"

"I just saw Marta Serragno outside."

Deb's face reflected the shock Rose felt. "*What?* You *saw* her?"

"Yes." But why would Deb be so shocked? Unless she knew about Marta's anger toward Rose and had reached the same conclusion that Rose had.

"But that's crazy," Deb said. "What would she be doing here, of all places?"

"I don't know." Rose's dread increased. If Deb's reaction was this strong, it only confirmed Rose's suspicion that Marta would stop at nothing to "get back" at Rose. Marta must have said something to her. "When was the last time you saw her?"

"I—I—" Deb shrugged. "I'm not sure. Probably a week or so."

"Did she say anything about me?"

Deb gave a laugh that was a little too forced to be believed. "No, of course not. Why would she?"

"She was really angry at me the last time I saw her," Rose understated. "I thought she might have said something to the rest of the staff."

"Oh." Deb laughed. "No, she didn't do anything

like that. Actually, she's seeing some new guy, so she's been in a really good mood. I'm sure she's forgotten whatever it was that she had against you."

It was kind of Deb to try to reassure Rose, but her efforts only served to make Rose even more nervous. If Marta had moved on, it was even more incongruous that she was here.

But Rose didn't want to let Deb know that she was still worried. Clearly her friend was uncomfortable enough with the situation. "I'm sure you're right," Rose said with a smile. "In fact, that probably wasn't even her."

"You're right, it probably wasn't," Deb said quickly. "She wouldn't come to a place like this. You know she barely ventures down below the seventies in Manhattan."

Rose smiled and nodded, but the pit of her stomach ached. Something strange was going on with Marta, she just knew it, and she was going to have to guard against whatever it was.

She was still gnawing on the issue late that night when everyone had left and she was getting ready to lock the place up. When she was filling the straw dispenser, a knock at the door startled her and she dropped the straws all over the floor.

She saw it was Warren, and her apprehension was quickly replaced by another kind of jitters.

"What are you doing here?" she asked as she turned the lock and opened the door.

"Nice greeting."

"I'm not in the business of being nice."

He looked at her and smiled. "Yes, you are."

"Yes, I am." She crossed the floor and went behind the counter to pick up the straws she'd dropped. "So, seriously, what brings you here at this hour?"

"I've got a couple of things to go over. I hear business is going great guns, so I need to stay on top of things for Doc."

She glanced at him. "It's really not what you want to be doing, is it? Spending all your time here instead of working on your own business."

He gave a shrug, then said, "Coming here has its perks."

"Yeah?" She raised an eyebrow. "Like what?"

His blue gaze settled on her like a warm blanket. "Your excellent pie, for one thing."

"Ah." She nodded and tossed a handful of straws into the trash can. "You're not the first man to tell me that."

"No?"

She stood up and untied her apron. "Nope. I've even been told my apple pie is irresistible."

A small smile tugged at the corner of his mouth. "Magic, according to some sources."

Her heart pounded. She hung the apron up, then leaned on the counter in front of him. "You don't strike me as the kind of man who believes in magic."

"I never did before," he said, in a low voice that

made her feel as if a thousand butterflies were flying in the pit of her stomach.

"That's probably wise."

"Probably."

She looked at his mouth, then, embarrassed to be caught, looked back into his eyes. "And now?"

"Now…I don't know, maybe I've changed."

Kiss me, she thought irrationally. *Please kiss me.* "Have you? Changed, I mean."

He took a long breath, then said, "You ask a lot of questions."

"You *raise* a lot of questions."

He touched his hand to her cheek and ran his thumb absently along her jaw. "So do you, Miss Tilden."

This was dangerous. *He* was dangerous. And not just because he was great-looking, with those movie-star looks and football-player body. Because he was charming. His voice was like liquid, his gaze electric. She wanted him, but she didn't *want* to want him. Warren Harker had a long list of women in his past, and Rose didn't want her name added to that list.

"Do you want some coffee?" she asked abruptly, trying to break the mood.

He looked surprised. "Coffee?"

"Uh-huh." She turned to the coffeemaker. "I thought I'd make some before I go home. You in for a cup?"

"Sure," he said, still sounding somewhat bemused. Then he added, under his breath, "And a cold shower."

She smiled to herself and took the filter out of a drawer. "I could splash you if you want."

"I think you just did."

It was a delicate flirtation, in danger of escalating quickly. It'd already happened several times.

"What the—"

Behind her, Rose heard Warren get up and cross the floor. She turned to see him. "What?"

"There was someone out there."

Her stomach tightened. "There was? Over on the corner by that old building?"

He gave her a sharp look. "Yes. Have you seen someone hanging out there?"

"As a matter of fact, I have." She sighed. "This morning, I saw Marta Serragno over there."

"Marta Serragno?"

Rose nodded. "Deb was here with me, but she didn't see her. In fact, when we talked about it, I had all but convinced myself it was my imagination, but it's been bugging me all day. But now…I think it was really her."

Warren frowned. "Why would she be here?"

"Because of me. Because she has a vendetta against me."

"That's crazy," he said, then, looking as if he'd realized how cold that had sounded, he asked, "Was she alone?"

"No, she was with some man."

"So maybe she was on a date."

"He didn't look like her type."

"What did he look like?"

"Big, brawny blond guy. Looked like a body-guard. Or a linebacker."

Warren's expression was serious. "Blond guy? Did he look like that actor Nick Nolte?"

She thought about it. "Yes, he did, as a matter of fact. How on earth did you know?"

Warren's jaw was set in a hard line. "Just a lucky guess."

"Come on, Warren, you're making me even more nervous. Who is that guy?"

He tapped his fingertips on the counter. "If it's who I think it is, he's a real estate developer."

"Like you."

He shrugged. "Sort of."

"I don't like the sound of that."

"I don't like the sound of any of this. What, ex-actly, are you thinking Serragno has in mind?"

Rose looked at him, then recalled the scene with Marta and the man. She was sure that Marta had been looking in the direction of the diner. "I think she's planning to do something to sabotage me or my work here," she said. "I think she realized that she hadn't been quite thorough enough in blacklisting me and now she wants to finish it."

Warren looked interested. "Is she really that vin-dictive?"

"I've known her to be determined," Rose said.

"When she decides she wants something, she doesn't give up easily. For example, I'll bet she continued to try and contact you after the party we catered."

"She did." He nodded. "A lot."

"That's because she had her sights set on you." Rose pointed at him. "And *you* didn't comply."

"So maybe she's heard I'm here and she's out to get me, too?" He grinned.

"You laugh, but I wouldn't put it past her. See, it's a perfect example of how she operates. Determined."

"And now you think she's determined to cause trouble for you?"

"I think it's possible."

He came over toward her. "Don't worry. She won't hurt you. She can't."

Rose nodded. "You're right. She might try, but she can't *do* anything more than what she's done already. I'm probably just being too paranoid." And she decided, as she said it, that it was true. She *was* being paranoid. It wasn't as if Marta were going to try to hurt her physically. All she would do is try to get her fired. Big deal. Doc wasn't going to fall for that.

"Look," he said, "if it would make you feel better, I could hire a guard for you."

"A private bodyguard?" She turned back to the coffeemaker with a laugh. "Oh, no, no, no. I don't want some guy hanging around me all the time."

"So…do you have a guy hanging around some of the time?"

She threw a glance over her shoulder. "I assume you don't mean that in the creepy way it came out."

He laughed. "I mean do you have a boyfriend?"

"Why do you ask?"

"Just curious."

"Are you willing to answer the same question?"

"Sure. I'm uninvolved at the moment."

"Good," she said, then quickly added, "Given how we…you know…" Her face flushed with the memory of their kiss.

"Kissed?" he asked with amusement.

"Yes."

"Then I assume you're similarly unencumbered?"

"Yes. At the moment."

"Is there anyone in particular that you're interested in?" He came up behind her and put his hands on her shoulders.

Her muscles melted beneath his touch. "Now who's got all the questions?" She moved to the freezer, hoping the cool air would cut the heat that was rising in her. She took the can of coffee out and scooped some of the fragrant grounds into the filter. "Strong?"

"Not strong enough to resist you."

"I bet you say that to all the girls," she said, scooping in more coffee with her shaking hand.

He put his hands back on her shoulders and turned her to face him. "No, I don't. You've got the magic touch, Rose. I don't know what it is, but you seem to have some sort of power over me."

It was all she could do to resist falling into his arms. "I need to put water in the machine," she said unnecessarily, reaching for the carafe and pouring the water in.

"Rose." He reached out and took her arm, pulling her to him. "Why are you avoiding this?"

Her breath caught in her throat. "Avoiding what?"

"This." He lowered his mouth onto hers.

It was bliss.

The scent of him, mingling with the aroma of the ground coffee, was a powerful aphrodisiac, and she drank it in, trying to ignore the danger of getting involved with a man like Warren.

His mouth moved against hers, reducing her resistance by degrees. He drew his finger gently down her cheek, then cupped his hands behind her head, holding her gently but firmly, kissing away her objections.

Rose forced herself to draw back. "We shouldn't do this."

"Probably not." He kissed her again.

She sank into him. It wasn't his will she was fighting but her own. And she was powerless against her own desire.

He moved his hands lightly down her sides, sending thrills of pleasure in the wake of his touch.

But a flash outside the window stopped them cold.

"What was that?" Rose asked. "Lightning?"

Warren was already at the window. He looked at the sky. "It's a clear night." He frowned and squinted at something in the distance, then muttered an oath. "It was a camera flash."

"A *camera flash?* Why?"

"I don't know," he said, his voice tense.

Something about his tone made her even more uneasy. "Photographers take your picture all the time, don't they? Surely this isn't *that* unusual for you." Not that she wanted a picture of her locked in a compromising position making any of the newspapers that were regularly interested in Warren.

"Photographers take my pictures at events. I've never been stalked for one."

This was all just too crazy. "Are you *sure* it was a photographer?" She went and stood next to him in the window. "Look, there's a streetlamp that's gone out. Maybe that was what we saw."

He looked up at the streetlamp. "Maybe," he agreed. "Tell me, when you saw Marta and that man earlier, were they taking pictures?"

The question surprised her. "No. At least…I don't think so." She searched her memory, but she had been so focused on Marta's sharp facial features that she could have been holding a basket of puppies and Rose wouldn't have noticed. "I don't know."

He appeared to consider this, then turned to Rose. "What about your sisters? Have they said anything to you lately about seeing anyone strange hanging around?"

"Sis*ter*," Rose corrected. "And how do you know about her?"

"I had you investigated," he said simply, looking back out the window. "When I thought you were trying to get information on me."

"You had me *what?*"

He looked at her, surprise etched in his features. "I had you investigated. Background check, that sort of thing."

She was shocked. She had never dreamed anyone might be checking into her background. And even though she didn't have anything to hide, the very idea of it made her extremely uncomfortable.

Warren must have seen that in her expression because he said, "Don't worry, it wasn't anything deep or invasive. He just did the usual surface check. You know, he found out when you and your two sisters were taken to the Barrie Home, and when the one sister was adopted, then where you went to school and your job history. It's not like he interviewed former boyfriends or anything."

But Rose could barely hear him, because she was still stuck on one word. "Adopted?"

"What?"

"You said my sister was adopted. But I live with her. I've always lived with her."

"Lily. Yes, I know about her. I mean the other one. Laurel? Is that her name?"

Rose's mouth felt dry. "I hate to tell you this, but your investigator can't be very good."

"What are you talking about? He's the best. And I have the invoices to prove it."

"I only have one sister," Rose said, but her voice was barely a whisper of uncertainty.

Warren frowned, then understanding came into his eyes. "Oh, my God, Rose. Rose, I'm so sorry. I—I shouldn't have been the one to tell you. And to tell you that way…I'm so sorry."

She looked at him, but could barely see him through the tears. "Are you sure?"

"Positive." He nodded and gently led her to a booth where she could sit down. "I'll give you everything George gave me. George Smith, that's the investigator. In fact, if you want, I'll put him back on the case. It's not the sort of thing he normally does, but I'm sure he'd do it."

"Laurel." Rose tried the name out on her tongue. It felt strange *because* it felt familiar. As if she'd known it all along.

Which was crazy, because she hadn't known it all along and, to her knowledge, she'd never even suspected that she had another sister.

"Yes. Laurel Standish." He heaved in a long breath. "No wonder George said you hadn't been in touch for years. I'd assumed it was some sort of falling out, not that you didn't know about her at all."

A sister. Laurel. Laurel Standish.

Lily, Rose and Laurel.

It sounded right.

She looked at Warren and he said, again, "I'm sorry."

She shook her head. "Don't be." A smile bloomed in her heart. "If it weren't for you and your paranoid poking around, I might never have known about her."

He laughed, clearly relieved that she wasn't angry. "So I'm forgiven?"

"This time." She smiled broadly. "This is the most amazing thing that's ever happened to me. And it's all because of you." She looked at him soberly. "Thank you, Warren."

"Anytime I can help by doing some paranoid poking around, I'm glad to." He reached out and stroked her hair. "Want me to call George and put him back on the case?"

"Yes. Well, wait. I have to talk to Lily." Her mind raced suddenly. She hoped Lily would be home when she got there. Lately, there had been a lot of late nights at the Hotel Montaigne. If Rose had to wait for Lily, she thought she might just burst.

"But can you do me one more favor?" she asked Warren.

"Anything at all. " He splayed his arms. "Name it."

"Can you give me a ride home? I don't want to wait one second longer than I have to, to talk to my sister."

He gestured toward the car. "No problem at all," he said. "Let's go."

Chapter Eleven

Rose had to wait almost an hour for Lily to come home. When she heard the key in the door, she jumped off the sofa and ran to the door, throwing it back while Lily stood on the other side, hand frozen in midair where she was working the lock.

"You will *not* believe what I found out tonight."

"I hope it's that you won the lottery and we can quit our jobs and go lounge on an island somewhere, being served drinks by handsome cabana boys." She put her coat and purse down in the hall and dragged herself into the living room. "Man, I don't think I can take many more of these fourteen-hour days." She sat down and put her feet up.

"Lily." Rose could barely contain herself. "I have something to tell you."

Lily immediately looked alarmed. "What's wrong?"

"Nothing's wrong. It's—" Suddenly she didn't have the words. "I don't even know how to start."

"Spit it out, sister. You're making me nervous."

"Okay…we have a sister."

Lily looked sharply at Rose and suddenly the fatigue was gone from her face, replaced with tense alertness. *"What?"*

Rose nodded. "We're not twins. We're—we're two of three triplets." She smiled. "It turns out that we have a sister who was adopted from the Barrie Home early on, when we were too young to remember."

Lily frowned, then waved the notion away. "No way."

"I'm seriously, Lily."

"But that's crazy. We'd *know* if we had a sister." Her face reflected all of the shock and confusion Rose had felt upon hearing the news. "Someone would have told us, wouldn't they?"

Rose shrugged. "Who?"

"Sister Gladys. Virginia Porter."

"Not if they thought it would hurt us. Sister Gladys never would have said or done anything that would make us, or any of the other kids, unhappy, no matter what. Mrs. Porter, too. Maybe there's even some ethical code or something that would prevent it, I don't know."

Lily shook her head, still trying to put the pieces together. "You need to back up and tell me how you know this." Her voice wavered, and Rose felt her own strength dwindle. "I want every detail."

A lump lodged in Rose's throat, and she tried to keep her composure long enough to get the story out. It wasn't easy. By the time she was finished, both she and Lily had tears streaming down their cheeks.

"We've always felt like something was missing," Rose said through her tears. "Maybe it wasn't just our parents, though. Maybe we knew, somewhere inside, that Laurel was out there."

Lily sniffed and nodded. "We must have. But why hasn't she tried to find us?"

"How do we know she hasn't?"

Lily gave a laugh. "We're not exactly hidden."

"I don't know about that. Our last name isn't the same as hers, and if Mrs. Porter and Sister Gladys aren't talking..." She shrugged. "Maybe they're not even there anymore."

Lily nodded her agreement. "So what do we do?"

"We find her. No matter what it takes." Rose's heart was simultaneously heavy and light. She wanted so badly to meet their other sister, but at the same time, more than two decades had passed. Something told her this wasn't going to be easy.

* * *

The next day, Rose was walking to the diner when a dark car with no license plates came screeching out of nowhere toward her.

Fortunately, she heard the revving engine when it was still a block away and had the presence of mind to hurry to the sidewalk. Unfortunately, the driver didn't seem to have any compunction about driving *onto* the sidewalk.

He was *trying* to hit her.

Terror lodged in Rose's chest and for a split second she was paralyzed by the fear. It was only at the last moment that the car swerved through an oily puddle, splashing her coat with filthy water. As she leapt out of the way, she lost her footing and fell against the building. The car sped off, leaving her breathless and wet, but alive and relatively unharmed.

Dick, who was pulling up in his car for his morning coffee, was the first on the scene.

"What the hell was *that?*" he growled. "Are you all right?" He knelt by Rose and put a surprisingly tender hand on her shoulder. Dick had always been so gruff in the past.

"I think so," she said, taking a fuzzy inventory of the various aches and pains the experience had left behind. "My ankle is killing me."

"How's your head?" he asked, sounding concerned. "Did you hit your head at all?"

"No. It's okay. Thanks."

"Come on, let's get you inside." He helped her up and carefully eased her toward the door.

"What's going on?" Stu asked, walking around from the alley.

"Some damn fool nearly ran our Rose down, that's all," Dick snarled. "And if I ever get my hands on the son of a—"

"Thanks, Dick," Rose said, smiling, even though she was feeling anything but happy. "I'd like to think it was just some sort of mistake."

"It was a mistake, all right."

Stu wordlessly fumbled with the keys to open the front door, then ran into the bells on the door with a loud clatter in his effort to make room for Dick and Rose. Before long, Hap and Tim had showed up, too, and all of the men insisted Rose put her foot up in a booth and relax while they took care of things. Even Dick volunteered to make the coffee, which was a good thing since it was far better than Hap's.

Eventually, they let Rose totter into the kitchen and cook, but they insisted she sit on a stool while doing so and ask for help every time she needed something instead of trying to get it herself. She appreciated their kindness, but by midday their doting was driving her crazy.

It did, however, give her time to think about what had happened, and the fact that it had been clearly deliberate. The car had been sleek and expensive, a Town Car or something like it. She hadn't been able to see the driver through the tinted window, but his maneuvers through the street and onto the sidewalk made her think this wasn't just some crazy drunk on his way home from a long night of partying.

It was Marta, she thought. It had to be. That bad feeling she'd had when she'd seen the woman out front had never entirely gone away. Now, with this happening, she was sure Marta was gunning for her. She never would have dreamed Marta would go so far, but the evidence was just too strong to ignore.

When Deb came in, Rose decided to pull her aside and tell her what she suspected. She didn't want to, but if Deb was still working for Marta and Marta found out about it, Deb might be in the same kind of trouble Rose was.

"Rose," Deb said, after hearing the story. "I hate to say this, but I think you're a little paranoid."

"I hope so," Rose said tersely. "But I thought I should warn you, just in case."

"Thanks, but I'm not afraid of Marta Serragno."

It was hard not to feel stung by Deb's dismissal of Rose's fear, but she reminded herself that the story *did* sound implausible, but if there was even a *chance* she was correct, it was her moral obligation to warn Deb. Now she'd done so. And even though Deb had blown it off, she had at least heard what Rose had to say, so she'd been forewarned.

Rose could only hope that some small part of Deb, at least, would take it seriously.

* * *

Warren hadn't planned on returning to the diner that day, but where Rose Tilden was concerned he was finding that things didn't tend to go according to his plans.

That really turned out to be the case when he walked into the restaurant and was informed by both Stu and Tim that "someone had tried to kill Rose."

"Where is she?" he asked sharply. He knew he had to get the story directly from her, rather than relying on the testimony of the two witless busboys.

Tim's face went red in the vehemence of Warren's tone, and he said meekly, "She's in the kitchen."

Warren wasted no time in going to the kitchen and asking, "What happened?"

Rose looked up at him, surprised. "I'm okay, thanks, how are you?"

"Rose, I'm serious," he said, with too much urgency in his voice. "What happened? Tim just said someone tried to kill you. I hope to God he was exaggerating."

She must have recognized that he wasn't in the mood for kidding around, because she sobered immediately. "I was walking in this morning and when I was almost in front of the diner, a car came racing out of nowhere and deliberately splashed me with dirty water."

He looked her over. There were small cuts and bruises on her face and arms. "And it hit you?"

She shook her head. "No, the ground did. And the wall, when I fell. The car kept on going down the street." She hesitated then added, "I think Marta is behind this."

His response was quick. "I don't think so."

She frowned. "What are you saying?"

He let out a long breath, but it alleviated none of his tension. He couldn't tell her the truth.

"Warren, are you saying you know who *is* behind it?"

This was ugly, and it was just getting uglier. "I'm not sure. But I have my suspicions. Obviously the security detail I've hired hasn't done the trick, so that leaves only one choice. We have to close the diner before someone else gets hurt."

"Close the diner?" she repeated incredulously. "Are you nuts? After Doc told us how much it means to him, how it's been in his family all these years? After he *specifically* entrusted us to take care of it while he was laid up so he'd have it to come back to?"

Warren shook his head. "I think Doc would rather we close up shop than take the chance on someone else getting hurt."

"I'm not sure about that," she argued. "Doc wouldn't want anyone to get hurt, obviously, but we don't *know* that anything else is going to happen. We can't even be sure that what happened to Doc and what happened to me this morning are related!"

He was tempted to ask *Now who's nuts?* "Well, I'd just as soon not have another dangerous, potentially unrelated event."

"No way." She was obviously putting her foot down. "We can't do that to Doc."

"It's safer."

"Maybe. But maybe not. And it would ruin the business."

"It would only be temporary."

She gave a humorless spike of a laugh. "When was the last time you heard of a restaurant taking a little sabbatical and coming back to good business?"

She was unyielding, which made this twice as hard for Warren. He knew what was going on. He could never prove it in a court of law, but he knew Larry Perkins of Apex was behind this. It was exactly his kind of scare tactic. The warning was clear: *Change your plans or kiss your friends goodbye one by one.* Over the years, Warren had heard a lot of rumors about Perkins's hand in development changes. But he'd never had to worry about how it might affect his own loved ones before, because he'd never had loved ones. He wasn't close to anyone, so no one got hurt. No parents, no wife, no children.

He was untouchable.

Until now. He had been observed spending time with Rose, and last night he had been photographed kissing her. That was all Perkins needed to start the ball—or the car, in this case—rolling.

And even though was wrong about Warren's relationship with Rose—they weren't really involved and in fact probably wouldn't ever see each other once this time at the diner was over—now that he *thought* there was something to it, Rose was in danger.

Which meant that if anything happened to Rose, it would be Warren's fault.

And he didn't want anything to happen to her.

"You're determined to keep it open?" he asked.

"Absolutely." She was resolute. Her delicate jaw was set determinedly, and her gaze was even.

He exhaled slowly. "Fine. But I want you to be careful. And I'm going to tell everyone else around here to do the same." He shook his head. "I think it's damn foolish to stay open."

"Duly noted."

"And ignored."

"Not ignored," she said. "Just…noted. Filed." She smiled. "But I promise you I'll be careful. Look, don't think for a minute that I'm stupid enough to *want* to risk my neck. I realize that what happened today was unusual and almost certainly deliberate. That bothers me. But I let the police know, and I don't know what else I can do. Closing the business of a man who trusted me to run it just doesn't seem like a reasonable option."

"Even if the people behind this are gunning for you specifically?"

She frowned. "You need to tell me exactly what you know about this before I can answer that. Come on." She sat down on one of the counter stools and patted the one next to her. "Sit down and spill it. Then we'll talk about what to do next."

Chapter Twelve

Warren looked at Rose for a long moment before sitting down. "Okay." He let out a long breath, then leaned his elbows on the counter and turned to face her. "You know how Doc said, at the hospital, that he was told by his attacker that this had something to do with me?"

She nodded.

"The building across the street from the diner," he went on, gesturing toward the large picture window. "I bought it recently. It's a prime piece of real estate and a lot of developers have been trying to get their hands on it for a long time."

"What do you want the building for?" Rose asked.

Warren tapped his fingertips on the counter. "You're not the only one who wants to know."

Well, that was no answer. "Are you going to tell me?" She hoped he would trust her, since for him this was clearly a matter of trust, but she didn't have any reason to offer why he should, apart from the fact that she knew he could.

Another long moment passed before he said, "I'm making it into luxury apartments. That's the short answer. And that's the reason everyone wanted it. It's a great location for people who work in the city but can't quite afford to live the way they want to in Manhattan."

"Makes sense." And that much of it did, but she still wasn't getting where the threats came into this. "But once you've bought the property, why would anyone bother trying to strong-arm you?"

"The guy I suspect is behind this has a reputation for doing just that kind of thing. And he's been gunning for me for a long time. It's just that he never had any leverage against me until now." He looked into her eyes and she saw a warmth in his that made her heart flip.

"And what does he have now?"

His mouth cocked into a half smile, but there was no humor behind it. "He thinks he has you."

Her stomach clenched. "Why?"

"Because he thinks *I* have you." His words sent her heart thrumming again. But it wasn't only Warren that did it this time, it was also fear. "That flash that went off when we were kissing…. I'm pretty sure that was the proof positive he was looking for before he decided who best to go after next." He gave a dry laugh. "He didn't want to run down the wrong person. That's his version of high morals."

Rose had heard of this kind of thing in bad TV shows, but she didn't think it ever really happened. "So this guy thinks you'll give up this multimillion dollar investment to keep me safe?"

Warren gave a nod. "In a nutshell, yes."

"That's crazy! Like a bad TV movie." But when put to that test, she realized, Warren had tried to get her to shut down another man's business and, presumably, hide in her house until the threat was gone. He hadn't made any more concessions than that. "So you knew that people were in danger because of your business dealings, innocent people, and you were so determined not to lose money that you let it happen?"

"No," he said firmly. "It's not about the money."

"Then what is it about? What could it possibly be about if you're willing to let people get hurt so you can bulldoze forward?"

"You can't let a guy like that win," Warren said, too patiently. "You can't reward those kinds of scare tactics. If I let him win, you can be damn sure that he would have gone after this property next."

"The diner?" she asked skeptically.

He shook his head. "The *property*. This is a valuable piece of land, or it will be once the building across the street is renovated. So what do you think, would Doc have sold?"

She started to see where he was going with this. "No," she admitted. "I doubt it." In fact, from what she'd seen of Doc, he wouldn't give the place up even if he were offered millions for it. It was a point of family pride for him; it was his heritage. He was a man who knew that was more important than anything.

And Rose, who knew nothing of her own heritage, was a woman who could really imagine how valuable that would be.

Warren continued. "So a guy who'd have an old man beat up, then have a woman run down with a car—what do you think a guy like that would do to an old man who wouldn't sell him his old diner?"

She shuddered to think. "I don't know." She wasn't even sure she wanted to know.

"He'd have him hurt, that's what. Him, Esther, you, Hap, Tim, Stu," he counted them off on his fingers, "*everyone* here, everyone he figures Doc cares about. And Doc's list is a hell of a lot longer than mine."

Rose longed to ask him if she was truly on his list, or if all of this came from a feeling of obligation since he'd been caught kissing her and therefore had put her in harm's way.

But she couldn't ask that.

For one thing, she was too afraid of what the answer might be.

She didn't have any business hoping Warren Harker was falling for her. He knew, as well as she did, that they came from two different worlds. And he looked to be a man who felt even more strongly than she did about keeping those worlds separate. After all, he never brought friends or associates here. Whenever he came to the Cottage, he came alone. And he left alone.

"So what does it all mean?" she asked. "What next?"

"Next? I leave. You take care of the diner now. You handle everything until Doc gets back. It shouldn't be long. He's making strides every day."

"So you're just going to leave it all to me to take care of?"

He shrugged. "It's that or stick around and create the impression that I have deep feelings for you."

His words stung her. "Oh, you wouldn't want anyone to think anything like *that*."

"No," he said seriously. "I wouldn't." He gave her a lingering gaze before adding, "I'm going now. If there's an emergency, you have my card, but otherwise…" He put his hand out. "It's been pleasant working with you."

It was a complete brush-off. She couldn't even believe it. After everything they'd been through together, all the time and energy they'd spent trying to keep the diner in business, and those kisses… After all that, he was putting his hand out and saying it had been "pleasant working together," as if they had been just business partners. Or associates. Or even just acquaintances.

That's what she felt like, an acquaintance.

She didn't shake his hand. Instead, she just looked at it, then looked at him and said, "Thanks."

He dropped his hand by his side. "You'll call if you need me?"

"I won't need you," she assured him.

But she did need him. That was what she couldn't tell him, especially now that he'd told her he was staying away. But she needed his sporadic visits, she needed the rush of adrenaline she got when she saw him coming through the door, she needed the lift she felt when he flirted with her and the ecstasy she felt when he kissed her.

It hadn't been long since he'd come into her life, but for some reason she didn't know what she was going to do when he'd left it.

"I'll be fine here," she went on, demonstrating a coolness she definitely didn't feel. "Don't worry about it."

"Good," he said a little stiffly. Was it too much to hope that he might be sorry to not see her anymore? "Then I guess our business here is concluded."

She couldn't bear to look at him. If she looked at that face, into those eyes, there was the distinct danger that she would break down in tears, and she did *not* want to do that in front of him. "Yes, it is," she said, hoping she sounded light. "Thanks for your help."

She had the sense that he didn't know what to do with himself as he was preparing to leave, but that could have just been wishful thinking on her part. Perhaps the awkwardness she felt was all her own.

She watched him get his coat and go to the door. She didn't move. She didn't speak. Even though it felt as if her whole soul were being pulled out along with him, she didn't budge.

And when he was gone, part of her felt as if he'd taken her soul with him. Because she knew he wasn't coming back. He'd said he was ending his association with her and with the restaurant.

And if there was one thing she'd already learned about Warren Harker, it was that he was a man who stuck to his word.

"So let me get this straight," Lily said incredulously. "You let him just walk away? The one man who had a detective on the case, who had found out about our sister and who had perhaps the best connections in the world to find her? You just let him walk away?"

Rose felt like crying. "What could I do? He said he was disassociating himself. It wasn't like I could *make* him stick around."

Lily looked at her closely for a moment, then said, "Maybe you could have, if you'd told him exactly how you really feel about him."

Rose looked sharply at her sister. "What are you talking about?"

"A-*ha!* If I didn't know it before, I'm sure of it now. You're in love with the guy!"

"I am not!" Rose objected, but even she didn't believe the half-hearted objection. "I barely know him."

"You know him well enough to have shared not one but *two* steamy kisses."

They *had* been steamy. "That doesn't mean anything."

"For you it does, little sister. I can't remember a time when you've kissed a man without a fair idea that the relationship had the potential to go somewhere. That's just not like you. So you kissed him because you thought you had something going."

"Well, we don't," Rose snapped.

Lily laughed. "And you're saying that because he had the unmitigated gall to distance himself from you so thugs who wanted to hurt him didn't do it through *you*. Because they know he cares about you."

"I'm afraid that's a major oversimplification."

"Doesn't matter, the bottom line's the same. You're not going to tell the guy you love that you love him, and we're not going to get to use his detective to find our sister. Now, the first thing I can't do anything about, because you've made up your bullheaded mind about it, but the second thing we can get to work on."

Rose still wasn't feeling all that optimistic. "Finding Laurel?

Lily nodded. "Now that we have her name, it can't be that hard to trace her on the Internet. So pull yourself together. First thing tomorrow, we're going to the public library to try and find out what happened to our long lost sister."

The next morning they did go to the library, but they had little luck in investigating Laurel. After entering several credit card numbers in order to purchase information, they learned that Laurel had been working as a nurse in private hospitals in New York. She'd married once, about five years ago, but the marriage had been dissolved within three months.

After that, all they could trace was a job she'd had in a physical therapy center in upstate New York until about a year and a half ago. After that, she seemed to have dropped off the face of the earth.

By the end of a long day of research, Rose and Lily left feeling as if they didn't know much more about their sister than when they'd gone in, but they had learned two important things: first, she existed. That was important, since they hadn't known about her at all until now and it was hard to take just one man's word for it. Second, they'd learned that Laurel had worked as a nurse. And though she'd disappeared, it didn't appear that she had died, since they had been able to do a thorough—and nervous— check of the social security death records.

All of which left them feeling as if it were good news and bad news. But at least now they knew she was out there. And both women vowed that they would not give up until they'd found their sister.

A week after he'd left the diner never to return, Warren showed up at closing time. Rose had come to expect that, usually, when he came it was late, so initially she had looked for him at closing time. But after the last time he'd left, she hadn't expected him to come back.

But when he finally did, he made no pretense that it was a social visit.

Chapter Thirteen

"Hi," Rose said, feeling a flush rise in her cheeks. Her heart reacted even faster than her brain, and it banged so hard she was half-afraid he might be able to hear it. "What brings you here? Not that I'm complaining. It's nice to see you again."

She hoped, hoped, hoped that he'd come to see her. That this past week without seeing her had been as difficult for him as it had been for her. Unfortunately, that didn't seem to be the case.

"Has anything else happened?" he asked Rose without preamble. "To you or anyone else?"

She cast a careful glance at Deb, then whispered, "No, and, please, I don't want everyone here getting all psyched out about it. As it is, Deb has been on edge for days."

He frowned. "Why?"

"Because of the car trying to run me down and you going around making all that noise about the possibility of more things happening."

"You warned her to be careful, right?" he asked, searching her eyes.

"Yes, of course, but I think that's what's got her so nervous. Look, Doc isn't going to be back for another week and if Deb quits on me, I don't know *what* I'm going to do. You should have seen this place earlier. It was packed."

"Good news for Doc," he said tersely.

"But bad news for the rest of us?" she asked. "Obviously you've got something on your mind. Why don't you just tell me what it is."

He moved closer to her and put his hands on her arms, looking deeply into her eyes. At first, he didn't say anything. Then one moment stretched into two, stretched into three and he finally said, "Perkins, the guy I was telling you about before, sent me a generous offer for the property."

"I don't understand."

He spoke in a quiet voice, but with conviction. "It's like the nocturnal animal coming out during the day. You know something's wrong. You *know* he's a threat. And he lets you know that by coming right out in the open."

Rose glanced at Deb, who was setting up tables. "Hey, Deb? Why don't you go on in the kitchen and finish making those apple pies you were working on? I'll take care of that."

Deb glanced nervously at Warren, who still had his hands on Rose, then asked, "Are you sure?"

"Of course. Go on, I'm starving, so I can't wait to try a piece." Rose watched Deb go into the kitchen, then turned back to Warren and said, "So this guy has confirmed he wants the building and you feel his doing that is a threat."

"Exactly. So please," he tightened his grip on her arms, "please, just this once, close up the place for the rest of the week. Just until I can get a formal announcement together for the press. Once the plans are out there, Perkins loses his power over the deal."

"Then why on earth didn't you do that before?"

He released his grip. "Because I can't just come out with incomplete plans or a blueprint that might be completely different from the final property. Plus, there's zoning to think about and—" He shook his head. "Trust me this once, would you Rose?"

She looked into his eyes and was struck by the intensity she saw there. He was begging her. "I do trust you," she said quietly. "But I just feel like you're overestimating the danger here. You're from a polite society uptown, where no one knows their neighbors and people don't look out for each other. I know you can't understand it, but it's just not like that here."

"I understand it better than you think," he said, so softly she almost thought he hadn't actually said it.

"What are you getting at?"

He let out his breath in one long hiss, and sat down in the booth, gesturing for her to do the same. "The Barrie Home."

She sat. "What about it?"

"I spent the first six years of my life there."

She felt as if she'd been punched in the stomach. All this time they'd had this one thing in common, yet she'd had no idea. She'd shaped all of her ideas about Warren based on a completely erroneous assumption.

"The Barrie Home," she confirmed, thinking she must have misunderstood him. "Right here, in Brooklyn."

He nodded. "Tilden Street. When I met you and you told me your name and where you were from, I figured out pretty quickly that we'd come from the same place. Just not at the same time."

"But why didn't you say anything?"

A long moment passed before he said, "It's not something I talk about much."

"Why not? Does it embarrass you?"

He looked surprised. "No. Embarrass me? Are you joking? Hell, I'd give anything to have never left the place."

"I don't understand."

He leaned on the counter and looked straight

ahead as he spoke. "I'm not the kind of man who likes to dwell on the past or whine about it. So, suffice it to say, life with my adoptive parents was…difficult."

The sounds of Deb's banging around in the kitchen punctuated the silence that followed.

"I don't want to pry," Rose began carefully. "But do you want to talk about it?"

He looked weary. "My father, the man who adopted me, didn't want children. He agreed for the sake of his wife. And to be fair, I doubt he knew he would grow so jealous of the time she had to spend caring for a child. But his jealousy took the form of emotional abuse…"

He told his story.

Rose's heart broke as she watched his face, listening to his stories of abuse by the man who had been entrusted with his care when he was only six. For all the years that Rose had wished she and Lily *had* been adopted, listening to Warren made her see that perhaps things had worked out for the best for her, after all.

She only wished she could go back in time and comfort the child who had grown into the man in front of her now. To soothe the pain that had etched scars into his soul.

"What about your mother?" Rose asked when he had finished. "Didn't she try to protect you?"

He flattened his hand and tipped it side to side.

"She had her own problems. She drank too much. I guess she was just trying to cope with him, too."

"I'm so sorry," was all Rose could think of to say.

"Don't be. It was hard, but it made me the man I am today."

"And are you happy?" she asked earnestly.

He looked at her solemnly. "It can be lonely, but I'm basically content."

"You don't *have* to be lonely."

He reached across the table and put his hand on hers. "I decided a long time ago that it wouldn't be fair to subject a woman to my lifestyle full-time. I'm always working, never in one place for too long."

"Are you saying you wouldn't be satisfied with just one woman?" she ventured to ask.

He gave a small smile. "Until recently, I thought I couldn't be."

"Then what happened?"

"Then I met you and I lost my head for a few days." He gave a soft laugh. "But you deserve better than me, Rose. You deserve a man who's ready to devote his whole life to making you happy."

Tears filled her eyes and burned like acid. "Shouldn't I make that kind of decision for myself?"

He looked pained, and he squeezed her hand before saying, "I'd love to be selfish and say yes, but I can't."

She had to gather her courage before she could ask, "Am I wrong in thinking you feel something for me?"

"No, you're right. I do. I feel more for you than I've ever felt for another woman. I feel more for you than I ever dreamed I could feel for a woman." His expression grew determined. "And that's exactly why, for once in my life, I'm going to do the right thing and be selfless."

"It's not selfless to make decisions for me," Rose argued. "It's not selfless to pull back because of how you *imagine* things *could* be. Give me the choice. Let me show you how it can really be." She took his hands in hers. "Please, Warren. Nothing in life is without risks, and nothing is as worthwhile a risk as love."

"I can't."

She couldn't believe this. She wasn't reaching him. He might be hearing her words, but he wasn't taking in anything she was saying. He'd already made up his mind, and that was that.

"Please, Warren," she said, knowing it was already a losing battle.

He looked her in the eye, gave a sad smile and said, "You'll thank me for this someday." He stood up to go.

"I won't beg," she said lowly, although if she'd thought it would help, she probably would have.

"You'll never beg, Rose Tilden. You're too good for that."

Tears pricked at her eyes. "So this is it? You're really just going to walk out on me, after everything I just said?"

This time, he didn't meet her eyes. "I've got to go. Please try to understand." He put his coat on and opened the front door.

The bells on the door jangled loudly.

"Rose?" Deb came running from the back. "Don't leave yet. Oh." She saw Warren and Rose standing there and must have put two and two together. "Pie's almost ready," she said to Rose.

Rose tried to smile politely. "Thanks, Deb."

Warren took advantage of the distraction and said, "Goodbye, Rose. I'll keep my investigator on the case and let you know when he finds something out."

"Thanks," she said, but it was barely a whisper.

"Meanwhile, call if there's an emergency."

There was an emergency. Her heart was breaking over a man she could swear loved her, too. A man who *thought* he was doing the best thing for her, but who actually didn't have a clue.

She'd only just found out how wrong her assumptions about him had been, and now he was making them about her.

A more pessimistic person would have taken that as a sign.

"Where'd Mr. Harker go?" Deb asked, coming out of the kitchen, wiping her hands on her apron.

"He's gone."

"Is he coming back?"

"No. I don't think he's ever coming back."

"I'm sorry," Deb said, twitching nervously. "I didn't mean to run him off."

"You didn't," Rose said, trying to collect herself. She didn't want to seem too pitiful, but at the same time that was exactly how she was feeling. "I did."

"Do you want to talk about it?" Deb asked hungrily, clearly angling to get all the dirty details.

"No." Rose sighed heavily. "To tell you the truth, I'd rather just go home."

"But my pie." Deb's face fell and her voice took on the tone of a four-year-old who hadn't gotten her way. "I wanted you to try it and tell me how it measures up. I used your recipe. Well, pretty much. I added a couple of my own things."

Rose didn't want to hurt Deb, but the last thing in the world she felt like doing was sitting around eating pie with her. "Would you mind terribly if I took a rain check? I'll try it tomorrow."

"But it's fresh out of the oven *now*."

There was no arguing with her, Rose could tell that right away. Deb had been talking about this darn pie all day long, and the only way she was ever going to get home was if she just went ahead and tried some of it.

"Sure," Rose said. "What the heck. Maybe it will make me feel better."

"Oh, goody!" Deb clapped her hands. "Now, you sit down right there and I'll run into the back to get it. Don't move!"

"I won't." She was not in the mood for this. At all. She sat down at the counter and put her elbows on the cold Formica. Then, while she waited for Deb, she sank her head into her hands and thought about Warren.

Theirs had been a tumultuous relationship, but their chemistry had been undeniable. And recently she had really begun to feel close to him in a way she'd never felt with another man. She'd felt as if maybe he could be The One.

Now, maybe that was crazy romantic fantasy, but she felt it right down to her soul.

And she thought he felt it, too. In fact, he'd told her tonight that he *did* have feelings for her. So her instincts had so far been right.

But then he'd left. And no amount of begging, pleading or crying would have stopped him, so she was glad she hadn't really done any of that.

"Here you go," Deb announced, coming out of the kitchen with a plate. "You are my first guinea pig."

Rose picked up the fork Deb had brought on the plate and gave her a wry look. "You might not want to use those terms in presenting your cooking in the future."

"Oh." Deb giggled. "You know me…"

Rose cut a piece off and put it in her mouth. It was…odd. Sort of acrid.

"Well?" Deb asked eagerly.

"It's good," Rose lied.

"Have another bite!"

"Okay." She took another bite off the slice. The second one was even worse than the first. It was as if she'd accidentally spilled dishwashing liquid into it.

"Good, huh?" Deb asked excitedly. "I really, *really* want to be able to do it as well as you."

"Well, it's—it's close."

"Have some more."

"Okay." Rose was beginning to feel a little queasy. She wasn't a food snob, but this was beyond the pale. She wished Deb would return to the kitchen, so she could subtly throw the remainder of the slice away.

"That's right," Deb said, watching her. "Eat it all up." Suddenly her voice didn't sound all that chirpy and eager.

Instead, it was cold. Hard. Commanding.

Frightening.

Chapter Fourteen

Rose was beginning to feel woozy. "I think I've had enough."

Deb smiled, a pasted-on sneer of a smile. "I don't think so, Rosie. It's your pie recipe. Don't you like it?"

"What did you add to it?" It was hard to form the words. Rose's mouth felt as if it were gummed up with glue.

Deb looked at Rose's plate, at the three-quarters-eaten pie, and said, uncertainly, "Oh, this and that."

"What was this—" Rose tried to stand up but lost her balance and sat down again "—and what was *that?*"

Deb scrutinized her for a moment, then said, "I'm kind of sorry, you know."

"Sorry for what?"

"You know, that I had to do this." She gestured vaguely toward the pie. "Marta made me and you know how hard it is to say no to her."

Things were fuzzy. Rose wasn't quite getting this. "Marta made you *what?*"

"Doctor the pie. You know. So that hunky Trump of yours will sell his building to her or whatever."

Rose grasped the countertop. The room was going dark. "Call 911," she said. "Please."

Deb shook her head. "Sorry, I can't do that. I was paid to do this job right."

"I pay you."

"I couldn't go to a fast-food restaurant on what you pay me." Deb gave a mean laugh. "No, *Marta* pays me. And like I said, this was her idea. Sorry."

Now, what was left of the room began to spin. Rose didn't know what was going on, but she knew she didn't have long. "What was her idea? What did you do?"

Deb looked at her. Or, rather, two Debs looked at her. Her vision was doubling, tripling by the moment. "Well, I guess you're far gone enough. It's not like you're going to tell anyone this story. Marta hired me to ask if you needed help, then told me to wait for my moment and add one of her crushed-up tranquilizers to your food." She shrugged. "I think it's to scare your boyfriend, but I'm not sure. I told Marta the less I knew, the better. With the paycheck she's giving me, I'd just as soon go to Mexico and forget this whole thing." She pursed her lips and looked at Rose. "But you were nice to me, so I really am sorry."

By now, Rose couldn't formulate words. She looked down and saw multiple counters containing multiple plates of apple pie. In one weak but angry gesture, she pushed the plate of pie off the counter and listened to it shatter.

"Oh, look. Now you've made a big mess that I'm going to have to clean up," Deb said. "Thanks a lot."

"Call…" Rose tried to reach her purse, which was only a few feet away from her on the counter, but she couldn't.

"You're not calling anyone, Rosie," Deb said, neatly lifting Rose's purse from the counter. "I can't take any chances. Now just go to sleep. It would feel good to go to sleep now, wouldn't it?"

Rose squinted at Deb and only then did she realize Deb was wearing the latex gloves Rose normally reserved for cutting jalapeños and the like.

She was trying not to leave fingerprints.

"What are you…" Rose tried to catch her breath, and to collect her thoughts. "What are you trying to do to me?"

But she didn't hear the answer. Before Deb could say a word, the world went black for Rose and she slid down the bar stool and landed with a heavy thunk on the cold linoleum floor.

* * *

Warren couldn't stand it. He hated how he'd left things with Rose. She'd put herself out there, right on the line for him, and instead of admitting how he really felt about her, he'd brushed her off.

And what was worse, she knew it. She knew exactly what he was doing and why he was doing it; she'd tried to talk him out of his stupidity but he'd been too stubborn to listen.

Well, he didn't want to be that guy.

Maybe Rose was right. Maybe he shouldn't be trying to protect her by not getting involved. Maybe the chances of someone getting hurt were comparatively slim.

And maybe, as she'd said herself, that was a chance worth taking.

He wasn't sure.

It had never been worth it in the past. Coming from the home he'd grown up in, Warren had learned very early on that you couldn't count on anyone, not even the people you were *supposed* to be able to count on through thick or thin.

Yet he and Rose had had plenty of run-ins and they still liked each other. They still respected each other.

And more to the point, she was still willing to be with him, even after butting heads with his bad side.

Warren looked out the window and watched the landscape turn from Brooklyn to Manhattan. And only then did he realize that he was *leaving* home, not *going* home. And the home he was leaving wasn't merely the town, it was the woman.

Rose. The woman who made him feel like himself no matter where he was. The woman who made him feel *accepted* for himself, no matter what that was.

He leaned forward and tapped on the glass separating him from his driver. "Denny," he said. "Turn around. I need to go back to the Cottage Diner."

"Yes, sir," the driver said, and he made a U-turn right in the middle of the road. If the police caught him, there would be a hefty fine, but Warren didn't care. He'd pay a million bucks in fines just to get back to Rose before she decided—or realized?—that he was a jerk who was completely unworthy of her.

The minutes passed like hours, and Warren drummed his fingers on the armrest. He watched the streets turn to the Brooklyn Bridge, and counted the rails as they passed over, waiting for the moment he would get back to the diner and hoping for all he was worth that Rose would still be there.

When the driver pulled up in front of the restaurant, Deb was at the door, fumbling with the keys.

Warren leapt from the car before it had fully stopped. "Is Rose still here?" he asked her.

Deb turned to him, sheer panic clear in her expression. "Who?"

"Rose."

"No. Uh, no. She left." She glanced reflexively inside the restaurant. "Hours ago."

Warren followed her gaze into the diner and saw, in the dim light, someone lying on the floor in front of the counter stools. "What's that?" he asked, more to himself than to Deb.

Deb's response was to run. Warren wasn't even looking at her when he suddenly heard her footsteps booming down the sidewalk.

It required no thought at all. He ran after her, catching up to her handily in a matter of seconds and dragging her back to the diner. "Give me the keys," he growled.

"But—"

"Give me the keys."

"Okay, okay." She took them out of her pocket and tossed them to him. "Take them. Let go of me."

He didn't release his grasp of her arm. "No way. You're not going anywhere. If anything—" He looked at her, and the heat of a thousand suns seemed to rise in his temper. "If *anything* has happened to Rose, I'm holding you personally accountable."

Deb tried again to wriggle out of his grasp, but he held firm.

Now he knew, without a doubt, that something had happened to Rose and if Deb hadn't done it herself, she damn well knew about it.

He worked the lock open with one hand and shoved the door open. The bells jingled loudly as the door hit the back wall.

"Let *go* of me," Deb was arguing.

He locked the door behind them and put the key back in his pocket. "Where's Rose?" he asked, tightening his grip on Deb's arm.

"I don't *know*." She struggled more.

"Bull." He dragged her across the floor to the light switch and turned it on.

Immediately he saw Rose lying on the floor.

He let go of Deb and ran to Rose. "Oh, my God. Rose." He knelt beside her and put a hand on her cheek. She was cool the touch. "Call 911," he barked at Deb.

"What's wrong?" she asked in a voice that suggested she knew a lot more than he did about what was wrong.

"You tell me," he said, retrieving his cell phone from his pocket with one hand while holding Rose's hand with the other. "You're the one who did this to her. What did you do?"

"I didn't do anything!"

"Tell me what you did and maybe the feds will go easy on you."

Then Deb began to wring her hands in front of her. "It wasn't my idea."

"What wasn't?"

"Hurting Rose."

"*What did you do?*"

She continued to wring her hands. "I added something to her pie."

"What was it?" Warren asked, clipping his phone shut after telling the ambulance where to come.

"Some sort of tranquilizer," Deb said. "Marta gave it to me."

"Marta Serragno?"

Deb nodded.

Warren looked down into Rose's pale face. "Hang in there, baby," he said, squeezing her hand. "Just a few more minutes." Then to Deb he said, "Is she working alone or with someone?"

"I don't—"

"Don't tell me you don't know. I've had an investigator following you. Tonight he told me you met with Serragno at the bridge. Who is she working with?"

"Some guy," Deb answered, sitting in a booth and dissolving into tears. "I don't know his name. Larry something. He's her boyfriend," she cried. "Please don't send me to jail. I can't go back."

He didn't need to ask what she meant. His investigator had already told him Deb had been arrested twice for theft, once on a felony charge. This was a girl who did whatever it took to achieve what she perceived as getting ahead. Given what had happened tonight, Warren doubted anything could stop her from getting what she wanted.

He heard sirens in the distance.

Relieved that help was arriving, he opened his phone again and called Mark Benning. He told him everything he knew about what had happened and Benning said he'd be right down with the police in tow. Not Deb nor Marta nor Larry Perkins was going to get away with this.

Looking down at Rose and holding on to her increasingly limp hand, Warren could only hope and pray that she would be the one who *did* get away with it.

Without thinking about Deb or the paramedics or the police or anyone else, he leaned down to Rose's ear. "I love you," he whispered. He kissed each cheek, then kissed her lips. "I love you," he said again. "Hang in there. You need to hang in there for me. You never let me off the hook very easily, so I'm not letting you off this time. You're coming back, Rose, because I love you and I need you, and now that I've found you, I will not live without you."

Rose came to in slow motion. She was aware of sound around her; even though she could feel the stark light of the room, she didn't know where she was.

She forced her eyes open, which was as difficult as if they'd been glued shut. "Lily?" she asked faintly.

"I'm here, hon." She felt a soft, cool hand on her forearm and recognized her sister's touch.

Even so, there was still only one thing on Rose's mind. "Warren said that he—"

"I'm here," another voice said, and she recognized it, after a moment's processing, as Warren's. "Don't wear yourself out, sweetheart, you've got time."

"Warren?" Her sluggish heart skipped a beat and, with a small fluttering of her eyes, she managed to focus on him. "Are you really here?"

He smiled that dazzling smile, and her heart made another move toward life. "I'm here. I'm not going anywhere."

"What happened…Deb? She…did something… to the pie."

"She poisoned the pie, and she's going to spend a long time in jail because of it," Warren said angrily. "They also got her little cohorts, Marta Serragno and Larry Perkins. What you've been through is awful, but it's ended the threats to everyone at the diner."

"Doc?"

"Started working there again yesterday. And you'd better get well soon because he's threatening to bring you some of his own homemade chicken soup."

Rose managed a smile. "Thanks for the warning."

He reached out and smoothed her hair. "Anytime, sweetheart."

"Did you really say what I thought I heard you say?" she asked after a moment. "When we were…I can't remember. I think when the ambulance came? Did you really mean what you said to me?"

"What?" Lily wanted to know. She edged into Rose's vision beside Warren. "What did he say?"

"I said I loved her," Warren said, without moving his gaze from Rose's. He smiled down at her, radiating such warmth she felt it bloom in her heart. "I told her she had to stick around because I can't live without her. Is that what you were talking about?"

Rose smiled, though her mouth was dry and cottony. "That's pretty much it," she said with a single laugh. "Did you mean it?"

"More than anything I've ever said in my life," he said, smiling. He held her hand tightly in his. "And now that you've come back to me, you're never going to be off the hook. I hope you know that."

"Yes, sir."

He reached into his pocket and took out the ring box he'd been holding on to for three days, ever since she'd come into the hospital. He took a large diamond ring out and held it in front of Lily. "You're as close as I come to asking a mother or father for permission to marry Rose. So what do you say?"

Eyes alight, Lily looked to Rose for confirmation before saying, "Well, I *guess* you can have her."

Rose laughed and Warren turned to her. "Rose Tilden, everything I have said to you about relationships has been idiotic. I don't want some other guy devoting his life to making you happy, I want to do it myself. And I promise you, with everything I am and everything I have, that you will be my first priority. So what do you say? Will you marry me?"

Rose didn't even have to think about it. "Yes," she said. "The sooner the better, as far as I'm concerned."

"Me, too," Warren said, with a broad smile. "I want to catch you before you change your mind."

"Not a chance," Rose said.

"All the same, I'd rather not wait." Warren bent down and kissed her. "I've already waited too long to find you. Now that I have, I don't want to spend another day without you by my side."

Epilogue

Rose's feet were killing her. She really should have bought better shoes, since it was her wedding day, but old habits died hard and she was still shopping in discount stores.

"What's wrong?" Warren whispered, standing next to her in the receiving line. There were so many people waiting to extend their congratulations that the line went out the ballroom door, but the people Rose wanted to see most were all right here.

"It's obvious her shoes hurt," Dick growled, as he approached. "What, couldn't you afford to get her a decent pair?"

Warren looked at Rose, bemused. "Is he right?"

She nodded, laughing.

"Take them off, for Pete's sake."

"But—"

"But nothing. It's your day. Do what you want." He smiled at her. "You've got a lot of luxury to get used to."

"I'll try." It was true. From now on, she was going to be living in the clouds over Manhattan with the most wonderful man in the world.

Better still, her family was about to expand. Warren's investigator had found her missing sister's latest address, and it was in Manhattan. She and Lily planned to meet her in a couple of weeks.

After the honeymoon.

Hap was next in line. He had worn a suit that looked as if it were forty years old and hadn't been ironed in all that time. It was a little tight on him, too, and Rose wondered affectionately if he'd even *worn* it in that time. She was honored that he was wearing it now, for her wedding.

"I'm so happy for you two." He beamed, and clapped Warren on the arm. "You're a lucky son of a gun."

"I know it," Warren said.

"You s-s-sure aaachoo!" Al took a handkerchief from his pocket and dabbed his nose. "Sorry," he said. "These flowers really set off my allergies. But it's worth it to see the two of you tying the knot."

Tim was next in line and he hung back, looking uncertain as to whether he should speak.

"Tim, thank you for coming," Rose said, reaching for his hands. "It wouldn't have been the same without you."

Tim blushed and said, "Gee, thanks." Then he said to Warren, "Congratulations."

"Thanks, Tim."

Stu and Paul were up next, Paul yawning and Stu calling Warren "Warner."

Finally came Doc. "You two," he said, putting a hand on Warren's shoulder and one on Rose's. "I can't believe things have turned out so great."

"It's thanks to you, Doc," Rose said, feeling her eyes fill with tears. "If you hadn't taken me on when no one else did, I wouldn't have met up with Warren again. You saved my life."

Doc chuckled. "I don't know, fate has a way of working things out. But I'm glad it all happened under my roof." He reached into his pocket and took something out. He handed it to Rose.

It was some sort of coin. "What's this?" she asked, turning it over in her hand.

Doc laughed. "Look at it."

She examined it more closely. It was indeed a coin, about the size of a silver dollar; only instead of having a monetary value engraved on it, it read Good For One Happily Ever After.

"Oh, Doc." She handed it to Warren. "Where on earth did you find it?"

"Someone gave it to Esther and myself more than fifty years ago," he said. "And it worked. I thought you two deserved the same kind of happiness."

"We'll treasure it," Rose said.

"Thanks, Doc," Warren added quietly. "That means an awful lot to us." He handed the coin back to Rose and she grasped it in her palm.

"So where are you two off to next?" Doc asked.

"I don't know, he won't tell me." Rose laughed. "I thought we were on the way to the airport when we ended up here."

"We're on the way now," Warren told her. "Honest."

"And where will we end up?"

"Now that's still a secret. But suffice it to say, there will be sand, and palm trees, and all you need to wear while we're there is sunscreen." He laughed. "Now, come on, let's get going."

"I'm ready!"

They went out to the waiting limo and the driver opened the door for them.

They climbed into the backseat and when they were settled, Warren tapped the glass and the driver pulled into the street while Warren poured two glasses of champagne.

"Here's to you," he said, handing one to Rose. "My wife. My life."

She smiled and clinked her glass against his. "To *you*." She dropped the coin on the little table with the champagne. "And to happily ever afters."

* * * * *

Don't miss Lily's story,
IF THE SLIPPER FITS
by Elizabeth Harbison
Coming in June 2006 to Silhouette Romance.

If you enjoyed what you just read,
then we've got an offer you can't resist!

Take 2 bestselling
love stories FREE!
Plus get a FREE surprise gift!

Clip this page and mail it to Silhouette Reader Service™

IN U.S.A.	IN CANADA
3010 Walden Ave.	P.O. Box 609
P.O. Box 1867	Fort Erie, Ontario
Buffalo, N.Y. 14240-1867	L2A 5X3

YES! Please send me 2 free Silhouette Romance® novels and my free surprise gift. After receiving them, if I don't wish to receive anymore, I can return the shipping statement marked cancel. If I don't cancel, I will receive 4 brand-new novels every month, before they're available in stores! In the U.S.A., bill me at the bargain price of $3.57 plus 25¢ shipping and handling per book and applicable sales tax, if any*. In Canada, bill me at the bargain price of $4.05 plus 25¢ shipping and handling per book and applicable taxes**. That's the complete price and a savings of at least 10% off the cover prices—what a great deal! I understand that accepting the 2 free books and gift places me under no obligation ever to buy any books. I can always return a shipment and cancel at any time. Even if I never buy another book from Silhouette, the 2 free books and gift are mine to keep forever.

210 SDN DZ7L
310 SDN DZ7M

Name	(PLEASE PRINT)	
Address	Apt.#	
City	State/Prov.	Zip/Postal Code

Not valid to current Silhouette Romance® subscribers.

Want to try two free books from another series?
Call 1-800-873-8635 or visit www.morefreebooks.com.

* Terms and prices subject to change without notice. Sales tax applicable in N.Y.
** Canadian residents will be charged applicable provincial taxes and GST.
All orders subject to approval. Offer limited to one per household.
® are registered trademarks owned and used by the trademark owner and or its licensee.

If you enjoyed what you just read,
then we've got an offer you can't resist!

Take 2 bestselling
love stories FREE!
Plus get a FREE surprise gift!

Clip this page and mail it to Silhouette Reader Service™

IN U.S.A.	IN CANADA
3010 Walden Ave.	P.O. Box 609
P.O. Box 1867	Fort Erie, Ontario
Buffalo, N.Y. 14240-1867	L2A 5X3

YES! Please send me 2 free Silhouette Desire® novels and my free surprise gift. After receiving them, if I don't wish to receive anymore, I can return the shipping statement marked cancel. If I don't cancel, I will receive 6 brand-new novels every month, before they're available in stores! In the U.S.A., bill me at the bargain price of $3.80 plus 25¢ shipping and handling per book and applicable sales tax, if any*. In Canada, bill me at the bargain price of $4.47 plus 25¢ shipping and handling per book and applicable taxes**. That's the complete price and a savings of at least 10% off the cover prices—what a great deal! I understand that accepting the 2 free books and gift places me under no obligation ever to buy any books. I can always return a shipment and cancel at any time. Even if I never buy another book from Silhouette, the 2 free books and gift are mine to keep forever.

225 SDN DZ9F
326 SDN DZ9G

Name	(PLEASE PRINT)	
Address	Apt.#	
City	State/Prov.	Zip/Postal Code

Not valid to current Silhouette Desire® subscribers.

Want to try two free books from another series?
Call 1-800-873-8635 or visit www.morefreebooks.com.

* Terms and prices subject to change without notice. Sales tax applicable in N.Y.
** Canadian residents will be charged applicable provincial taxes and GST.
All orders subject to approval. Offer limited to one per household.
® are registered trademarks owned and used by the trademark owner and or its licensee.

DES04R   ©2004 Harlequin Enterprises Limited

SILHOUETTE Romance

COMING NEXT MONTH

#1806 A TAIL OF LOVE—Alice Sharpe
PerPETually Yours

Marnie is a wire fox terrier with a mission: reunite his family.
With strategically placed canine chaos as his main tool, if he can get
the career-focused Rick Manning and the easygoing teacher Isabelle
Winters back together, he just might prove that dog is a *couple's*
best friend....

#1807 IN GOOD COMPANY—Teresa Southwick
Buy-a-Guy

A newly svelte Molly Preston has something to prove. And
"buying" former big man on campus Des O'Donnell as her date
for their high school reunion will go a long way toward righting
old wrongs. Or will it? Because not "winning" Des's love now
seems a far greater wrong.

#1808 SNOW WHITE BRIDE—Carol Grace
Fairy-Tale Brides

When Sabrina White runs away from her own wedding and arrives
on his doorstep in a blinding snowstorm, Zach Prescott's seven
nieces and nephews mistake her for Snow White. And though
Zach doesn't believe in fairy tales, this tycoon can't deny his
young charges a happy ending....

#1809 THE MATCHMAKING MACHINE—
Judith McWilliams

Loyal to her fired coworker, Maggie Romer seethes for revenge
upon the new boss, Richard Worthington. Writing a computer
program that analyzes Richard's preference in women, Maggie
wants to become her, seduce him and dump him! That is, until his
kisses show her that sometimes the best-laid plans of women and
machines can go deliciously awry!

SRCNM0